THE ZOMBIE APOCALYPSE SURVIVAL GUIDE FOR TEENAGERS

JONATHAN McKEE

The Zombie Apocalypse Survival Guide for Teenagers

Copyright © 2013 by Jonathan McKee

Publisher: Mark Oestreicher
Managing Editor: Anne Jackson
Editors: Kathryn Schoon-Tanis, Laura Gross
Design: Adam McLane
Creative Director: Daryl Dixon

All rights reserved. No part of this book may be reproduced in any form by any electronic or mechanical means including photocopying, recording, or in¬formation storage and retrieval without permission in writing from the author.

Scripture quotations marked NLT are taken from the Holy Bible, New Living Translation, Copyright © 1996, 2004, 2007. Used by permission of Tyndale House Publishers, Inc., Carol Stream, Illinois 60188. All rights reserved.

Scripture quotations marked NIV are taken from THE HOLY BIBLE, NEW INTERNATIONAL VERSION®, NIV® Copyright © 1973, 1978, 1984, 2011 by Biblica, Inc.™ Used by permission. All rights reserved worldwide.

ISBN-13: 978-098874-1355
ISBN-10: 0988741350

The Youth Cartel, LLC
www.theyouthcartel.com

Email: info@theyouthcartel.com

Born in San Diego
Printed in the U.S.A.

CONTENTS

ENDORSEMENTS

"Great strategies to outlast the zombies (who are coming), and apply ancient truths to obstacles we continue to face everyday."

—Ralph Winter, Hollywood Producer (*X-Men*, *Planet of the Apes*, *Lost*, *X-Men Origins: Wolverine*, and dozens more)

"The Zombie Apocalypse Survival Guide for Teenagers is awesome! Actually, it's brilliant. Part "The Walking Dead" and part survival journal, it is guaranteed to grab the attention of even the most jaded and bored teen, surreptitiously guiding them to think about life's most important issues. Want your kids to consider life from a biblical perspective? Give them this—it's that good!"

—Rick Johnson, bestselling author of *That's My Son*, and *Better Dads Stronger Sons*

"Jonathan's creative new *Zombie Apocalypse Survival Guide for Teenagers* is exactly the type of devotional teenagers will actually read. This resourceful little tool provides a captivating fictional story about three teenagers surviving against the odds, cleverly interjecting 27 sets of questions that drive young people to think deeply about decision-making, their morals, and truth from God's word. In a fun, interesting way, Jonathan helps teens tackle tough issues like coping with pain and depression, drinking, loving difficult people, and the temptation to indulge in fleshly desires. The teenage guys in my small group will be blown away that there's a Christian author who uses the popular post-apocalyptic fictional premise to address their real-life issues--I'm looking forward to hear their response."

—Doug Fields, Author, Speaker

"The most original student devotional I've ever read."

—Josh Griffin, LoveGodLoveStudents.com

ACKNOWLEDGMENTS

Thanks to God for being my source of hope when life seems hopeless.

Thanks to Lori who is the reason behind my smile!

Thanks to Alec, Alyssa, and Ashley not only for being my joy, but also for reading this book in the early stages and helping me cast direction for this project.

Thanks to my brother Thom for his creative vision, his countless ideas, and his encouragement to keep this book honest and real.

Thanks to Greg Alderman, Megan Leever, David R. Smith, Todd and Lynda Pearage, and my dad for reading this and giving me honest criticism. Your feedback was extremely helpful.

And finally, a huge thanks to Marko and Adam for believing in this project, not being scared of the word *zombie*, and taking the leap with me to make it happen when so many others were scared of the ramifications.

THE
SURVIVAL
GUIDE

WHAT YOU SHOULD EXPECT FROM THIS GUIDE

Zombies, strays, eaters, uglies . . . what are they called? It depends on who you ask. After all, it's not like there'd been some global communications effort to label them.

Fast, slow, lethal, clumsy . . . which are they? All of the above. Don't be too quick to make assumptions about them—it could cost you.

This isn't a normal book. It's not even a typical zombie survival guide. It's the story of three teenagers who endured and survived against the odds, adapting where many adults failed. To be honest, not many teenagers survived The Havoc either— probably because most of them didn't acclimate and learn like these three did.

For one thing, they didn't carry much in their packs: a crowbar, a pair of bolt cutters, a Bible and a few paperback books, a homemade grill made from a shopping cart, and a few other cherished items.

Does the fact that they carried a Bible surprise you? It was about the only thing that made sense after the rest of the world dissolved into chaos. And it served as a trustworthy guide when they were faced with some difficult choices—much like the choices you face today (but without any zombies, hopefully).

So what was the secret to their survival?

Good question. The answer lies in the following pages copied from Chris's journal . . . one of the few who survived.

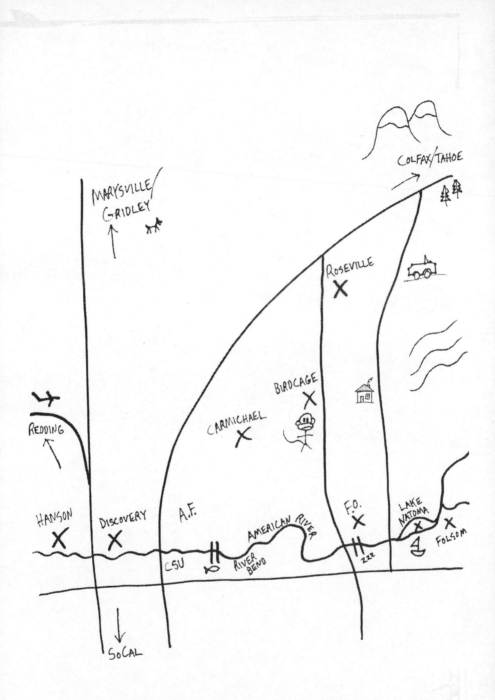

FOUR YEARS AGO THURSDAY

It's been almost four years since "The Havoc." That's what we call the zombie uprising. Although few use the word "zombie." We just refer to them as "strays."

It was the week of March 18, 2019. I remember the date because it was my 14th birthday. *Happy Birthday, Chris! Your dead neighbor is tearing through your fence and trying to eat your schnauzer!*

Most people were killed within the first month. And those of us who survived were now "learners." We noticed and adapted. In other words, it was basically just the intelligent people who remained. I'm just keeping it real when I say that. Most of the guys who bullied me in junior high are now corpses roaming around South Sacramento. (I know this for a fact because I dodged one of them when I was driving a Mazda that we hot-wired a couple of years ago. Somehow I resisted the temptation to put the car in reverse and back over him.)

After a couple months, shortly after the power grid went dark, my little brother Cody started keeping a calendar. I followed his lead and recorded key events, writing them on a stack of Applebee's placemats we'd found. That stack is now a journal of sorts.

Survival hasn't been easy for the three of us—Cody, Chelle (a girl who joined up with us two years ago), and me. Chelle lost her family and had no one. Cody and I shared some food with her, and days turned into weeks, which turned into years. We care for her like a sister now . . . but a cool sister, not the kind that hogs the bathroom.

It's surprising how many teenagers *didn't* make it. I figured they'd be better survivors than that—they were young, strong, and in better physical shape than most adults. But the majority of them died within the first month—not because of a lack of strength or endurance . . . more often it was because they were careless and irresponsible.

Somehow, the three of us survived.

And after the two-year mark, we began sharing our stories and some survival tips with people we met on the road. Not a lot of groups like ours have made it. I guess our little "family" is sort of an anomaly because we're alive and we still like each other.

A year ago now, David, my friend and fellow survivor, told me he really appreciated the survival tips we shared with him, and he suggested that I keep writing them down. Since then, I've been more diligent about recording what we've learned and documenting our story of surviving the last four years. I've used 60 placemats so far, and I've got only seven left. What follows is the story of our journey.

This coming Thursday it'll be four years.

Happy Birthday, Chris! You're still alive!

HEADPHONES LEAD TO HEADSTONES

Before The Havoc started, teenagers commonly wore head-phones. Undeniably, those were the first to become snacks for some wandering corpse.

Back during the first month of chaos, when we still had electricity, some teenagers kept wearing their headphones to get their Rihanna or Maroon 5 fixes. It didn't take long before one of those strays would walk right up behind them and . . . well . . . game over.

That almost happened to our friend Jake out by the Arden Fair Mall. Jake had those awesome Beats™ by Dre headphones with sweet bass. He and his buddies got up one morning and went from store to store, looking for food. This was when the stores still had a few canned goods sitting on random shelves. Jake was listening to some Kanye while he perused the aisles of an abandoned Target, so he didn't even notice that stray wandering around in the sporting goods department.

Jake's friend Mike was the first to spot the corpse from across the store. He started yelling for Jake, but Jake was lost in his music, nodding his head to the beat as he reached to the back of a shelf for a can of condensed milk. The stray headed right for Jake—it was one of the faster ones!

So Mike grabbed a cricket bat from sporting goods and sprint-ed toward Jake. The stray was almost within arm's reach of Jake when Mike embedded the bat into its jaw.

Needless to say, Jake doesn't like Kanye's music anymore. He actually gave up on wearing headphones altogether.

It's this simple: Your ears are one of your greatest defenses. Don't mess with your hearing. *Ever!*

Before all of this craziness started, my dad never liked earbuds or headphones of any kind. I never really understood his frustration. He thought headphones were nice to wear on airplanes or buses, but he didn't like it when we wore them around the house or at school. He called it "antisocial" and said, "Headphones just further the divide between teenagers and adults."

He was pretty adamant about it.

One day, Dad came home with two big boxes from Costco. "Chris! Cody! Here you go!" He'd bought each of us a big docking station for our iPods. It had big speakers and a remote.

"Play them as loud as you want. Just no headphones," he said.

I didn't really care. Speakers . . . headphones . . . it made no difference to me. Plus, it was a really cool docking station.

Looking back, I can see what Dad was doing. He liked the docking station because he could hear what we were listening to. That was a pretty smart move for a parent because some of my friends listened to some pretty bad stuff. Plus, with these new docking stations, we didn't block out the rest of the family with our headphones.

I kind of understand my dad's logic. My friend Sam always wore headphones. And it didn't matter where we were—at his house, the mall, or a football game—Sam always had music pumping in his ears. Whenever I tried talking to him, he'd pull one of the earpieces back and grunt, "Huh?"

So frustrating.

I like me some music, but come on.

It's funny how in this new world, teenage isolation is no longer a problem. Kids aren't alone in their rooms pumping music into their heads; instead, groups of people, like our little "family," gather together in the same room for safety and have actual conversations.

I guess that's something we can appreciate about this new world. It makes me wonder if my dad was right all along.

I miss my dad.

So if you should ever stumble across an iPod with a trickle of power left in it, think twice about putting on those headphones. Because today in this world, headphones lead to headstones.

JOURNAL ENTRY #1

///

Something to Think About
Back to Reality . . .

• Chris talked about teenagers' love for music. Name a few of the songs that you listen to the most.

• What's your favorite playlist (assuming that you have playlists)?

• Why do you think some young people prefer wearing headphones to playing music out loud through a docking station or on a stereo? Which do you prefer?

• What do you think about Chris's dad's statement: "Headphones just further the divide between teenagers and adults"?

• Name something you do that might "further the divide" between you and your family.

• In the new world, people don't isolate themselves but gather together and have conversations. What would it look like if families in our society today regularly gathered together for conversation?

THE BIBLE PROVIDES SOME GOOD WISDOM:

"Run from anything that stimulates youthful lusts. Instead, pursue righteous living, faithfulness, love, and peace. Enjoy the companionship of those who call on the Lord with pure hearts." (2 Timothy 2:22, NLT)

• What does this verse tell us to run from, and what are we supposed to pursue instead? How can we do these two things?

• Do young people ever put something in their ears that "stimulates youthful lusts" today? Give an example.

- What does this verse tell us to enjoy?

- How can you make an effort this week to meet with Christian friends or family?

SOMETHING I CAN DO THIS WEEK:

Think of some family or friends who are an encouragement to you in your faith. Take a minute right now to make plans to hang out with these people sometime this week. Open up a dialogue with them about what it might look like to "pursue righteous living, faithfulness, love, and peace" in your world.

WHY PROVERBS IS MORE RELEVANT THAN EVER BEFORE

About five years ago, just a few weeks before I turned 13, my dad shared a verse from the first chapter of the book of Proverbs:

"The fear of the LORD is the beginning of knowledge, but fools despise wisdom and instruction." (Proverbs 1:7, NIV)

I gotta be honest. Sometimes when my dad shared verses with me, it was boring. But for some reason, I can still remember this conversation like it was yesterday. We talked about wisdom, and we discussed examples of how we could make wise choices that week.

I walked away from that conversation with good intentions of seeking out God's wisdom.

And then I turned 13.

I don't think the word *wisdom* would accurately describe the way I acted as a teenager. Once I ate a whole cup of kitty litter—*on a dare!* I thought it would impress my friends. It just landed me in the emergency room.

At that age, *wisdom* wasn't really in my vocabulary. The words *impulsive* or *shortsighted* are probably better descriptions of that stage of my life.

That is, until the dead started walking the earth.

It's amazing how life-or-death situations tend to change every-thing. Now when we read the wisdom in the book of Proverbs, the words have a renewed meaning. Chelle probably wouldn't be with us if it weren't for that book.

A little over two years ago, Cody and I had a bad experience with a girl named Lindsey. We met her by the Delta, and she convinced us that she was hungry and needed our help. So we shared our food and let her stay by our campfire that night. When we woke up the next morning, Lindsey (if that was even her real name) was gone, along with Cody's backpack and my bow and arrow.

We were so angry with ourselves for being fooled and getting ripped off. Cody and I argued all day about what we should do the *next* time we encounter someone who seems nice and help-less. Cody swore he'd never trust another person on the road. I maintained that we should give the person a chance but guard our supplies more carefully. We never did resolve the issue that night. We were probably too angry to think straight.

Three nights later, Cody and I read these words in Proverbs 2:

"For the LORD grants wisdom!
From his mouth come knowledge and understanding.
He grants a treasure of common sense to the honest.
He is a shield to those who walk with integrity.
He guards the paths of the just
and protects those who are faithful to him.

Then you will understand what is right, just,
and fair, and you will find the right way to go.
For wisdom will enter your heart,
and knowledge will fill you with joy.
Wise choices will watch over you.
Understanding will keep you safe." (Proverbs 2:6-11, NLT)

The next morning while we were hunting duck, we met Chelle out on the levee by the old airport. She was famished and alone. Her clothes were tattered, and her long blonde hair was dirty and pulled back into a ponytail. I remember saying a quick prayer, "Okay, God, you said you grant us wisdom. Help Cody and me make the right choice here. Help us to do what is 'right, just, and fair.'"

Suddenly, Proverbs 25:21 popped into my head:

*"If your enemies are hungry, give them food to eat.
If they are thirsty, give them water to drink."*

So we shared some duck with Chelle . . . and the rest is history.

I'm so glad we gave Chelle a chance despite our bad experience with Lindsey. In a world full of strays, wisdom is the difference between survival and death. Wisdom is morality in a world where laws no longer govern.

Proverbs gives us guidance that is more useful than ever before. Rarely does a day pass when we aren't forced to make a decision that has consequences, good or bad, for everyone in our group. It's good to know these decisions aren't being made based on selfishness or some quick moment of fun. Our decisions are grounded in justice and righteousness that comes from a truth we hold close to our hearts.

I'm 18 now and the three of us read a portion of the book of Proverbs almost every night.

JOURNAL ENTRY #2

//

Something to Think About
Back to Reality . . .

• Chris confessed something he did on a dare that was really foolish. What's the most foolish thing you've done to impress someone?

• Chris claims the words *impulsive* or *shortsighted* are probably better descriptions of teenagers. Do you agree or disagree? Why?

• When life became dangerous for Chris and his group, they all became more interested in wisdom. Why?

• The author of Proverbs writes, "The fear of the LORD is the beginning of knowledge." What does that mean? And what does "fearing God" actually look like?

• The author of Proverbs explains that when we pursue God and the wisdom that flows from him, we'll understand what is right, just, and fair. Give an example of what this might look like in your life.

SOMETHING I CAN DO THIS WEEK:

Write out a specific example of something you can do to pursue godly wisdom. If it's a task, set a reminder in your cell phone or write it on your calendar. Once you've done it, talk with a friend or family member about what you learned from the experience. Set a time to do it again. Make it a habit.

KNOW YOUR ENEMY

Never assume.

That's what my dad used to tell me every time I jumped to a conclusion. Like the time I caught my first grounder during baseball tryouts when I was 11.

"Easy!" I pronounced.

My dad just smiled. "Chris, no ball ever comes at you the same way. One easy ball just means the next one is more likely to be difficult."

He was wrong. It was two balls later. The coach cracked it hard; it hit a lump of grass on the ground and jumped up with a spin. I misread the direction and underestimated its speed. The ball hit me right between the eyes.

Twenty minutes later, I was sitting next to my dad on the bleachers with a towel on my nose, trying to stop the bleeding. My dad refrained from saying what I know he wanted to say. *Easy, huh?*

Sometimes we don't learn lessons unless they hit us right in the nose.

Ever since that moment in sixth grade, I've tried to never assume. This little piece of wisdom has come in handy since The Havoc. None of the dead are the same.

Some of the first strays we encountered were bodies from the morgue down the street. We'd seen what was happening on the news, but it didn't seem real until we saw three corpses meandering in our cul-de-sac. One of them had a huge line of stiches across his chest from the post-mortem autopsy. These three were slow and clumsy. My neighbor Brian walked outside with a baseball bat and took them down with one swing each.

Brian's mistake was assuming they would all be like that. A little while later, one of the neighbors from the big yellow house around the corner walked into our cul-de-sac, saw Brian, and exploded into a full sprint. He pounced on Brian and bit his neck like a lion taking down a gazelle. Its movements didn't even look human; it looked more . . . animalistic and unrestrained. This creature began devouring Brian right before our eyes.

Our neighbor Steve ran over to try to help Brian. But then the stray—human in form, but not in movement—sprang at Steve so quickly that Steve didn't have a chance to defend himself.

That single stray took out eight people on my street before my dad finally arrived with his shotgun and blew a hole through its chest.

Until that day, I'd never seen anyone get shot. It was nothing like you see on TV. The impact of the shotgun slug sent the creature soaring backwards about 10 feet. But it wasn't over yet. When the stray hit the ground, it twitched like a squirrel after a car hits it, but the thing wouldn't die. Eventually, it tried to get up, so my dad put another slug in its torso.

More twitching.

Walt, from the big two-story at the end of our cul-de-sac yelled, "Headshot! Take the headshot!"

My dad agreed. He pumped the action one last time, pointed the barrel right at the creature's head, and pulled the trigger.

The end result was much messier than it was with the baseball bat, but the stray was definitely dead . . . or gone . . . or whatever it's called when they finally stop moving.

I committed these experiences to memory. In this world we must learn and adapt to survive.

In the early days we were constantly learning, so I began writing down what we observed. We learned a handful of realities about strays within the first couple months:

• They're unpredictable. No two strays move the same way. If they're old or have been dead a long time, then they're slow movers. But if they're fresh, like the neighbor from around the corner, then they're quick, agile, and extremely lethal.

• They have no sense of fear or life preservation. This is one of their scariest traits. They just keep coming at you. They're either really smart or really dumb, but they never quit. There's no shooing these things away.

• They always seem to be looking for food. They'll eat anything alive. A lot of the neighborhood dogs learned that the hard way during the first week of The Havoc. Sadly, a lot of my neighbors did too.

• Strays produce waste, but they don't know how to take off their clothes when they do. So they smell horrible. If you're downwind, you can smell them coming from more than 100 yards away.

• If strays are starving, they'll turn on one another for food, like coyotes or dingoes do. Similarly, if they're in a group and you shoot one of them in the leg, oftentimes a few of them will turn on their injured companion, going for the easy meal.

• It always pays to know your enemy. You never know when a small detail might shed light on a truth that could save your life.

JOURNAL ENTRY #3

///

Something to Think About
Back to Reality . . .

- What do you think Chris meant by, "Sometimes we don't learn lessons unless they hit us right in the nose"?

- What are some lessons that you didn't learn until they "hit you right in the nose"?

- What are some ways young people today are vulnerable to "danger" because they underestimate the consequences?

THE BIBLE PROVIDES SOME GOOD WISDOM:

"Be alert and of sober mind. Your enemy the devil prowls around like a roaring lion looking for someone to devour. Resist him, standing firm in the faith, because you know that the family of believers throughout the world is undergoing the same kind of sufferings." (1 Peter 5:8-9, NIV)

- How does this passage describe the devil? Why do you think the devil is described in this way?

- What are some ways the devil "devours" people today?

- How does the verse say we can resist the devil?

- Describe what "standing firm in the faith" looks like when you resist these temptations.

SOMETHING I CAN DO THIS WEEK:

Write down three ways that the devil might attack you this week. Then try to find a Scripture passage for each temptation—a verse that tells you the truth of the situation. For example, if the devil is going to tempt you to lust over sexual imagery, read Proverbs 5:18-23 and see God's amazing plan for sex in the context of marriage, as well as God's warnings about looking elsewhere for physical satisfaction (also see Matthew 5:27-28).

CELEBRATE BIRTHDAYS ... THEY MIGHT BE YOUR LAST

"What was your best day?"

Cody would always start the question game whenever we got settled around a campfire. He loved asking questions. Last night's question was, "What's the first thing you'd do if the power came back on?" Fun discussion. (I said I'd watch a movie while drinking something cold. Man, I miss overpriced, extra-large soft drinks on ice at the movie theatre.)

But today's question was to reflect on our best day. I'd just started thinking when Chelle chimed in, "My 16th birthday." As she said it, her words were choked with emotion. From across the fire, I could see her eyes welling up with tears.

Chelle didn't have much of a childhood. She never knew her dad, and her mom was an addict. So Chelle was raised by her aunt who had three kids of her own. Chelle always felt like an outsider in her aunt's home. The love she received was always leftovers and hand-me-downs, much like her clothes and her toys. The only new gift she ever received came from her grand-father before he died—it was a small stuffed monkey with long arms that would wrap around her and clasp together with tiny Velcro hands. She named him Fling.

Living in that dysfunctional house, Chelle felt like Fling was her only friend. In the dark, she would embrace him whenever she was scared, but especially when she heard her uncle come home after a night of drinking.

He was a mean drunk. Whenever he got drunk, he realized how pathetic his life was. And then he took it out on anyone in his path. Chelle could deal with the yelling and even the hitting. It was the touching that pushed her over the edge.

Chelle was eight the first time her uncle did unspeakable things to her. The abuse continued almost every night for two years straight.

She never told anyone about it because she was too scared. But apparently someone was looking out for her. One Friday night at 2 a.m., her inebriated uncle stumbled to his car, merged onto Highway 49, and played chicken with a semi-truck.

He lost.

It wasn't until two years after his death that Chelle finally told her aunt what the man had done to her. Her aunt went ballistic, called Chelle a liar, and eventually kicked her out of the house. Chelle went into foster care at age 12. She'd lived in three different houses before The Havoc started.

Needless to say, by the time The Havoc began, Chelle had experienced more havoc than any human being should experience in a lifetime. She was only 13.

Chelle, a particularly resilient and self-sufficient little girl, had survived by herself for two years. She'd encountered some other groups during that time, but she never trusted the men. (I don't blame her.) So she wandered around by herself most of the time, until she found us.

It took her a while to warm up to us. Don't get me wrong; she was polite and seemed truly grateful for the food and water we gave her, but she was always . . . *distant.*

A few months after she joined us, Cody happened to be working on his calendar when he proclaimed to no one in particular, "It's almost Valentine's Day!"

Chelle sighed and said quietly, almost as if she were talking to herself, "I'm going to be 16."

Cody heard her. "Your birthday is on Valentine's Day?" he asked curiously.

"Yep," Chelle replied, staring off into the distance.

I don't think she gave it another thought that day, but I couldn't stop thinking about it.

The next morning, I told Cody I needed to go scouting for supplies. We were bunkered in a nice house in Carmichael, right off the American River. The place I needed to go was only an hour's walk away.

Fifty minutes later, I saw it: an abandoned Toys-R-Us. A quick crank of my crowbar, and I was inside the back door. During the first year of The Havoc, we quickly acquired a few "must have" tools to survive: one was a crowbar, and the other was a pair of bolt cutters. Both were necessary if you needed to unlock doors and get to abandoned supplies that no one remembered.

The store was cluttered but surprisingly well stocked. I guess toys stores weren't much in demand in this era. The grocery store and drug store down the street were depleted of supplies. (We'd helped deplete those years ago.)

After about 15 minutes in the toy store, I found exactly what I needed and carefully made my way back to Cody and Chelle.

That night, we had a birthday party. Dinner was rabbit and orange slices. Cody and I sang "Happy Birthday" and presented Chelle with an orange slice with a birthday candle in it. (The cake mixes all had about a one-year shelf life. I'd checked. Plus, a cake was really hard to bake over a fire.) She laughed and blew out the candle.

That's when I handed her my present.

It was wrapped in pink Hello Kitty paper, which was all I could find in the store. She didn't open it at first. She just stared at the present for a while and then smiled and hugged it. With tears streaming down her cheeks, she thanked us.

"Don't thank me yet," I said, trying to break the tension. "You don't even know what it is. It could be lame."

She finally began to open it, carefully removing the tape and gently unfolding the paper. She peeked inside one end, but saw only brown fur. With a quizzical look on her face, she continued pulling back the paper, eventually uncovering the stuffed monkey curled up in a ball, his long arms wrapped around himself and Velcroed to his sides. She bit her lip as she unfolded the furry beast, running her fingers over the soft fur.

"Does it look like Fling?" I asked, breaking the silence.

"He's a little bigger." Chelle answered with a smile.

"Maybe he grew," Cody offered.

We all laughed.

"I know, right?" Chelle said, tightly hugging the gangly monkey.

I remember the moment like it was yesterday, and apparently Chelle did too.

"Definitely my 16th birthday. Best day by a long shot."

JOURNAL ENTRY #4

///

Something to Think About
Back to Reality . . .

• What's the best gift you've ever given to someone? What made it a great gift?

• What's the greatest gift you've ever received?

• Why was Chelle's stuffed monkey, Fling, so important to her when she was a little girl?

• Why did Chris make such an effort to get her that special gift?

• What did Chris's gift communicate to Chelle?

THE BIBLE PROVIDES SOME GOOD WISDOM:

"For the sin of this one man, Adam, caused death to rule over many. But even greater is God's wonderful grace and his gift of righteousness, for all who receive it will live in triumph over sin and death through this one man, Jesus Christ." (Romans 5:17, NLT)

• According to this verse, what gift does God give us?

• The verse says we can receive righteousness from Jesus. What is righteousness?

• When we put our faith in Jesus, God makes us right. Then we triumph over something—what does the verse say we triumph over? What does this mean?

SOMETHING I CAN DO RIGHT NOW:

Write a thank-you note to God for this awesome gift, telling him why you appreciate it.

DOGS TRULY ARE YOUR BEST FRIEND

Three nights ago, Chelle almost bought it. She truly would have died if it weren't for Slippery.

Slippery is our Labrador.

Let me back up just a bit.

Cody and I grew up with a dog named Buster. Buster was a schnauzer, and he was the stupidest dog ever. Our friends told us, "Schnauzers are a very intelligent breed." Well, not Buster. Buster was an idiot.

One of Buster's worst traits was his nervousness. He walked around the house with his uncropped tail between his legs, whining and looking around the room as if the ceiling might collapse on him at any moment. And whenever the doorbell rang, Buster peed—every time, without fail. *Ding-dong!* Puddle.

When The Havoc started, Buster didn't make it. Cody and I actually miss the stupid furball now. He was an idiot, but he was family.

That's probably part of the reason why we were so glad to encounter Slippery about a year and a half ago.

Cody, Chelle, and I were in a rural part of Marysville checking out some abandoned houses that the fires didn't reach. It's kinda pointless to call any part of Marysville "the rural part," because all of Marysville is pretty much rural.

Anyway, we came across this old alfalfa farm, and we noticed a bunch of strays moving pretty fast in a field, like they were chasing something. We snuck up real close, and we found 13 strays chasing a frisky yellow Labrador.

The Lab wasn't worried in the slightest. He seemed like he was playing a game with them. He'd crouch low, wait till the walking corpses came within a couple of feet, and then pounce to the side in a playful gait looking back as if to say, "Ha, ha! You missed me!"

Chelle whispered, "Slippery little sucker, ain't he?"

A few minutes later, the dog noticed us. He gave the strays the slip, navigated the tall alfalfa, and plopped down next to us. The ornery little pup seemed to know the difference between strays and humans, because he nuzzled right up to Chelle and let her scratch him behind the ears.

"Hey there, Slippery," Chelle whispered, now scratching his chest as Slippery rolled to one side. "You showed some mad skills out there in that field."

The three of us crept away from the farm with our new friend close at our heels.

That night, Slippery—the name stuck—joined us at our campfire. Cody said, "I don't think we have enough food to feed one more." And just like that, Slippery slipped away as though he'd understood what Cody meant.

Chelle hit Cody in the arm. "You hurt his feelings!"

But not five minutes later, Slippery pranced back to his spot by the fire with a ground squirrel in his mouth. He plopped down and began to devour the gangly rodent.

Chelle smiled at Cody. "I think Slippery can hold his own."

And Chelle was right. Slippery has never been a burden. Quite the contrary, actually. There were a few nights when we had nothing to eat, and Slippery provided a nice rabbit, dropping it at Chelle's feet. Slippery was amazing!

But his bark was probably his best asset. Like the other night, for instance.

It was storming outside and the rain was coming down hard. Cody, Chelle, and I had checked out an abandoned house down in Folsom, making sure no strays would surprise us in the middle of the night. I don't know how we missed it, but we awoke to find Slippery barking and nudging Chelle's arm with his snout. Cody opened his eyes just in time to see a stray stumbling toward Chelle who was curled up asleep on the couch.

We later figured out that it must have come in through a cracked door in the coatroom off the kitchen entryway.

Slippery pounced, planted himself between the creature and Chelle, and growled. But strays don't have any fear or common sense. They just keep heading toward what they want.

Cody sprung to his feet and embedded his machete in the stray's skull. Chelle was less than two feet away. As the decayed figure dropped to the floor, we all breathed a sigh of relief. Cody walked over and scratched Slippery's head. "Good boy."

Chelle hugged the dog so tight he grunted, clearly enjoying the affection.

Slippery was truly man's best friend—I mean, *woman's* best friend that night.

JOURNAL ENTRY #5

//

Something to Think About
Back to Reality . . .

• What do you think the group enjoyed most about Slippery?

• Why would it be nice to have a dog like Slippery in a survival situation?

THE BIBLE PROVIDES SOME GOOD WISDOM:

"Two are better than one,
because they have a good return for their labor:
If either of them falls down,
one can help the other up.
But pity anyone who falls
and has no one to help them up.
Also, if two lie down together, they will keep warm.
But how can one keep warm alone?
Though one may be overpowered,
two can defend themselves.
A cord of three strands is not quickly broken." (Ecclesiastes 4:9-12, NIV)

• These verses give several reasons why two people are better than one. Name them.

• This passage offers some great wisdom not only for survival, but also for a life of faith. How could two people be an encouragement to each other in a relationship with God?

• What are some of the ways we become overpowered by temptation, and how could a friend help us defend ourselves?

• Name someone who shares your belief in God and encourages you in your life of faith; someone who's "got your back" and helps you avoid being overpowered by temptation.

SOMETHING I CAN DO THIS WEEK:

Call this person and share what you learned from this passage of Scripture. Talk about how you can help each other in your faith journey. You could even make a game plan to read the same Scriptures or Bible studies each week and then text each other when you complete it. Make plans to be there for each other during times of temptation or discouragement. After all, *two is better than one.*

LIFE WITHOUT TACO BELL

It's not like you can just stop at the Taco Bell drive-thru when the dead are walking the earth.

Food is hard to come by; so when you find some, you have to think several meals ahead.

In the early days, we used to devour food whenever we found it. Hunger conquered any shred of wisdom. Our bodies were used to getting three meals a day . . . *and snacks in between!* Now we thank God if we get one meal a day.

I remember when we could microwave a plate full of Hot Pockets. (I miss those delicious little morsels.) Now we have to chase our food.

Cody literally "chased" our food all around the valley a few weeks ago. Slippery was off on his own hunting expedition, and the three of us were walking along the old paved bike path that runs alongside the American River. Two turkeys ran across the path not 10 yards in front of us. Cody pulled out his bow, looked at Chelle, and said, "Watch this."

He pulled the bow string tight, fixed his aim, and then with a quick exhale released the arrow. It was a perfect shot—right through the neck of the fatter tom. And that's when the most peculiar thing happened. The turkey, now with an arrow sticking through its neck, stopped, looked at us, and then took off running down the path.

Chelle and I burst out laughing. "Watch what?"

Cody sighed and took off running after the resilient creature.

I don't know what he wanted more: dinner, his arrow, or his pride. But Cody chased the bird for about three hours before he finally brought it back to us . . . with two more arrows sticking out of its feathered back side.

Apparently the first arrow had hit the fatty part of the neck so perfectly that it hadn't phased the bird. That shot was one in a million.

Cody has become quite skilled with a bow. It's not that guns and ammo aren't available to us; it's just all about stealth. When you use a gun, you have to contend with the gun's report, which can be heard for miles around. Any humans in the area will know that something has been shot. In our world, a gun's report is like a dinner bell, so we opt to use bows and arrows whenever possible.

Hours later, when we were eating the delicious fowl, we reminisced about a time when we could just open the fridge, pull out some sliced turkey breast, and put it on a slice of bread. We haven't had bread in years.

Turkey is a real treat; that is, after you shoot it, defeather it, and spend an hour or two getting the fire just right to cook it. Turkey meat is hours in the making—and sometimes it's also hours in the chasing. When Slippery is there, he usually helps us with the chasing part.

Turkeys are a pretty rare these days. When The Havoc first started, it wasn't uncommon to see a handful of turkeys wandering in the fields by the American River. We'd find turkeys, deer, rabbits, geese . . . you name it. But once Wal-Mart wasn't open for business anymore, we started hunting to survive. All of that to say—we hardly ever come across a deer or turkey anymore.

One of our staple meals is actually rodent. Our friend Dan, a fellow survivor, taught us how to make a rat trap out of an old five-gallon bucket by burying a bucket up to its rim and drop a little leftover meat into it. It doesn't take much. We could literally use a shred of squirrel meat no bigger than a penny, and it would draw a rat.

Next, we'd place a small flexible branch across the top of the bucket, so it barely dipped down into it. Rats won't hesitate to use the branch as a ladder to lower themselves into the bucket. But when they step off the branch, it springs back up. Now the rat can't climb out of the bucket because the sides are too slippery.

Rat meat is pretty tasty when you cook it right.

Bugs are another staple food. They're easier to catch than large game or rodents, they're full of protein, and they don't require any cooking. Chelle had survived almost solely on bugs before we met her. She showed us several key spots to look for them, like under the bark of a fallen tree. When I asked her where she learned that trick, she simply smiled and told me, *"The Lion King."*

It's as simple as this: food is precious. Cherish it when you find it, save some of it if at all possible... and when the opportunity arises, share it with someone else.

JOURNAL ENTRY #6

///

Something to Think About
Back to Reality . . .

• What's your favorite fast-food restaurant, and what do you normally order there?

• If you had to cook a meal for your family at home, what would you make?

• Chris mentioned how he used to eat three meals a day as well as snacks in between, but now he's lucky to get one meal a day. Are there people in the world today who are in that situation? How do many of them get food?

THE BIBLE PROVIDES SOME GOOD WISDOM:

The Bible reminds us to take care of the poor and the hungry. For example, when the crowds came out to hear John the Baptist talk, he told them:

"Prove by the way you live that you have repented of your sins and turned to God. Don't just say to each other, 'We're safe, for we are descendants of Abraham.' That means nothing . . ."
(Luke 3:8, NLT)

He went on to say:

"If you have two shirts, give one to the poor. If you have food, share it with those who are hungry." (Luke 3:11, NLT)

• John tells the people to prove they are true followers of God by the way they live. What are some ways we can prove our commitment to God? (For example, see verse 11.)

• What are some efforts people can make to help the hungry?

• What's something you could do to help the hungry?

SOMETHING I CAN DO THIS WEEK:

Look for opportunities to help someone in need. Some situations aren't planned; you'll just see an opportunity and act on it. But also consider planning a time to serve. Call your church and offer to help with a project; offer to help by doing something that uses your skills. Serve at a local food pantry and help distribute food to the hungry. Talk with an elderly person who doesn't have many people to talk with. Schedule one of these activities and put it on your calendar.

BOOKS ARE THE NEW TV

Five years ago, many people would have scoffed at the idea that books are entertaining. But now that the power grid has been down for almost four years, you won't get much resistance from teenagers about this one. They don't have any electronics to distract them.

When the power first went off, we tried all kinds of stuff to keep ourselves entertained. Cody and I are big movie fans, so we'd act out scenes from our favorite movies. Cody has an amazing memory. He can act out entire scenes from any of *The Lord of the Rings* movies word for word.

I remember one night, shortly after we met Chelle, Cody stood in the firelight and reenacted a scene between Gimli and Aragorn:

"Toss me."

"What?"

"I cannot jump the distance. You'll have to toss me." He paused. *"Don't tell the elf."*

"Not a word."

Cody's movie impressions are always good for a laugh, but as days without power turned into weeks without power, reading became a much more desirable pastime.

We quickly learned to look for books in homes and stores. But they aren't as plentiful as you'd think. First of all, fires ravaged most of the suburban houses. (When the government's attempts at global extermination took place during the first few weeks of The Havoc, most of the firemen were too busy eating each other and didn't bother to do their jobs so fires raged out of control worldwide.) And second, as I already mentioned, only the smart people remain. Most of them are readers, so a good book is in high demand.

Between the three of us, we've got a collection of more than 20 books right now—mostly paperbacks because they're lighter and easier to carry. We've ditched a few as we've come across others. For instance, we were all quite happy to throw away *Twilight* the second we found something better. And that wasn't too difficult. Chelle discovered a copy of John Grisham's *A Painted House*. Great book! None of us had heard of it before, but now we read it at least once every few months—it's one of our favorites.

We've learned about survival from some of the books. I found a copy of *Into the Wild*. It's the true story of a young man who left civilization behind and went to Alaska, where he tried to survive on his own. We learned quite a few lessons from that book, like being prepared if we shoot some game, and which plants to avoid. Personally, I just hope to avoid ending up like he did.

Cody likes anything written by Robert Ludlum. He's found three of his books in the last year. It's amazing what you can find on people's bookshelves.

Chelle loves *The Great Gatsby*. That's one book she'll never trade. (Although I really don't get why it's a classic.)

But I have to admit that the Bible has probably become our top pick. Cody and I never got much out of the Old Testament back when we had a TV and other distractions. Now we've read the entire Bible several times. It takes us about a year to get through it because we spend time discussing what we've read.

No other book is filled with so much wisdom and life-changing guidance.

Reading together has helped us bond as a group. Cody and Chelle always want to talk about what we've read right as we're falling sleep. I think it's just because they want to stay awake a little longer. The nights can be scary.

JOURNAL ENTRY #7

//

Something to Think About
Back to Reality . . .

• What's the best book you've ever read? Why do you like it?

• If you could carry only five or six books with you for the rest of your life, which books would you take? Why?

• Why do you think Chris's family found so much help in the Bible?

• What wisdom have you gleaned from the Bible?

THE BIBLE PROVIDES SOME GOOD WISDOM:

"[The LORD said,] 'Study this Book of Instruction continually. Meditate on it day and night so you will be sure to obey everything written in it. Only then will you prosper and succeed in all you do.'" (Joshua 1:8, NLT)

• This verse calls the Bible the "Book of Instruction." How often are we to study the Bible and meditate on its teaching?

• According to the verse, what will result if we do this?

• How do you think someone who studies God's Word will "prosper" and "succeed"?

• What does prosperity and success look like for you? What does the Bible say prosperity and success look like?

• When could you or your family start reading the Bible this week?

SOMETHING I CAN DO THIS WEEK:

Open your Bible and read a chapter. If you don't know where to begin, start in the book of Matthew and read about the life of Jesus. Read Matthew 1 today, then read Matthew 2 tomorrow.

LOVE YOUR NEIGHBOR . . . AS LONG AS HE HAS A PULSE

My mom used to teach my brother and me to "love our neighbor." It took me a few years to figure out that she wasn't just talking about Mr. Detwiler next door. (He was kinda creepy.)

This principle of loving our neighbor seems a little weird now, probably because all of our neighbors are literally dead. And when a stray is sprinting toward your brother with no intention other than to eat him . . . love is the last thing on your mind.

But I'm pretty sure God wasn't talking about mindless creatures when he told us to love our neighbors. I think God probably meant we should love the people we encounter on the road. We frequently come across loners.

Just last week we saw a family with three young boys. They'd found shelter under the Sunrise Boulevard Bridge, and they were trying to spearfish some salmon from the American River. When they first saw us, the parents were scared and started yelling at us, "Get back!"

I don't blame them for being skeptical. Most of the survivors you encounter on the road these days aren't good people. They're like schoolyard bullies looking for an easy mark. Sadly, people have a little more to lose today than just their lunch money.

"Go away!"

We tried to calm them down. "Hey . . . no worries. We're just walking by. It's all good."

But Cody noticed that one of the little boys wasn't catching anything with his makeshift spear. Cody was never one to keep his mouth shut. So he walked over to the kid and said, "You're doing it all wrong. Here, let me show you."

Next thing we know, Cody is standing knee-deep in the water and giving those three kids a spearfishing lesson. "You don't just poke at it. If you poke, you're gonna miss. You might nudge them or prick them, but you aren't gonna catch anything," Cody held the spear tight and demonstrated how to do it. "When you jab at them, jab *through* them—straight through to the sand. That way if you get one, it can't slip off."

Cody caught a fish on his fourth try, and the kids shrieked in delight.

But the little boys were quickly distracted from the task at hand when they discovered how much Slippery enjoyed the water. One throw of a stick, and Slippery bounded through the water, swimming out and swiftly retrieving the floating stick in the slow current. For the next hour, Slippery fetched anything they threw, dropping the item at the boys' feet every time. Throw after throw, the pup never tired of the simple game.

The parents thanked us—especially since we caught their dinner. I think they felt a little guilty about yelling at us.

"Where do you guys stay?" the father asked.

"Various places," I responded truthfully. "Wherever it's safe."

"I hear that."

"I guess we've always hoped we'd find a community of survivors who've built a fortress of some kind to keep them out of harm's way," I confessed, thinking out loud. "Maybe that's just a dream."

"I've heard a few people mention a place like that around here. A hotel or something," the dad said. "Probably just a myth."

"When it sounds too good to be true, it usually is," I said.

Cody played with the kids for a while, but then we said our good-byes and went on our way. The parents echoed their thanks and gave us the biggest fish to take with us. One of the boys even ran up to Cody and gave him a hug when we began to leave.

"Do you have to go?" the little boy asked, looking up at Cody with huge brown eyes.

Cody squatted down to return the boy's hug, and then he added an affectionate noogie. "I do, little man! But I'm sure we'll see each other again."

It's a sacrifice to share food and supplies, but we always do it. Thanks to God's influence in our lives, we don't judge. If someone's hungry, we share. We've made lots of friends over the last few years: Water Tower Tim, Shotgun Mike, and Schizo Sam. You never know when you're gonna need a friend these days!

This principle of loving our neighbor has become really important to us. After all, it came straight from Jesus. Some guy went up to Jesus and asked, "Which is the greatest commandment?"

Jesus replied:

"'Love the Lord your God with all your heart and with all your soul and with all your mind.' This is the first and greatest commandment. And the second is like it: 'Love your neighbor as yourself.' All the Law and the Prophets hang on these two commandments." (Matthew 22:36-40, NIV)

That's pretty cool, if you think about it. The whole Bible is summed up in two things: love God and love others. Jesus demonstrated what that looks like throughout the books of Matthew, Mark, Luke, and John (Chelle's favorite Bible books).

I've found that one command flows from the other. The more we love God and allow him to influence us, the easier it is for us to love others—even those who are really hard to love.

Now, in the crazy world we live in, the principle of "love your neighbor" has serious ramifications. And we have plenty of opportunities to show love—just like we did with that family with the three kids last week.

I've seen plenty of survivors who don't know or practice these principles. To them, it's more about "survival of the fittest," and life is defined by a concept we learned in biology class.

Funny, not too many survivors are eager to help those people when they're in trouble.

Bottom line: Jesus knew what he was talking about. And the three of us will continue to extend love to anyone with a pulse—which isn't a whole lot of people these days.

JOURNAL ENTRY #8

///

Something to Think About
Back to Reality . . .

• Would you have stopped to help that family after they yelled at you? Explain.

• Who do you know that demonstrates what it means to "love your neighbor"? Describe that person.

THE BIBLE PROVIDES SOME GOOD WISDOM:

"Do nothing out of selfish ambition or vain conceit. Rather, in humility value others above yourselves, not looking to your own interests but each of you to the interests of the others."
(Philippians 2:3-4, NIV)

• Describe what selfish ambition and vain conceit look like. When are you tempted to act like that?

• What would it look like if we were to "value others above ourselves"? Write about a time when someone valued you and looked to your interests more than his or her own.

• Write about a time when you valued someone and looked to his or her interests more than your own.

• Chris proposed that loving God helps us love others because "the more we love God and allow him to influence us, the easier it is to love others—even those who are really hard to love." Explain this. Do you think he's right?

• How can we show love to God and allow him to influence us more?

SOMETHING I CAN DO THIS WEEK:

Write down something you could do to show love to a hard-to-love person this week.

INHERENTLY EVIL

It didn't take but a few days into The Havoc for us to recognize our true enemy in a world with no boundaries. With the police gone and the military scattered, bullies ruled the earth.

Survival of the fittest had proven more powerful than democracy. The big ruled the small.

Sure, strays were a nuisance and truly deadly at times, but they were like a Disney film compared to the living. I learned that when I lost my parents . . . but that's a story for another time.

Cody, Chelle, and I quickly learned to keep our eyes on our six (just like in *Call of Duty,* back in the day). It was easy to become preoccupied with finding food or making the perfect fire. But now we lived in a world where you couldn't drop your guard for even a second.

We learned that when we met Money's crew.

It's been a couple of years ago now, right before we got Slippery. But we remember it like it was yesterday.

The three of us had had a tiring day. Our traps were empty, and Cody's arrows missed every squirrel and rabbit that scurried past his sights. Once we'd finally settled down in a nice spot on the riverbank and lit a fire, a pack of strays arrived. So we had to abandon the fire, grab our supplies, and flee through the river to escape them. Miles downstream, we finally evaded the putrid-smelling creatures, and we plopped down by the shore, soaking wet and breathing heavy.

That's when we heard that distinctive sound of someone cycling the action of a shotgun, not five feet behind us.

We were either too tired or too scared, because none of us moved a muscle. We just laid there on the riverbank.

I slowly turned my head to see our aggressor. Seven men stood behind us wearing orange Folsom State Prison garb, an interesting fashion choice. At that time it had been almost two years since The Havoc had begun. So if they were prisoners, I wondered, why hadn't they changed clothes?

"Swimming?" the man with the gun inquired with a sardonic grin.

"Actually, I just sweat a lot," Cody quipped. "It's a problem I've had since puberty."

The gun bearer took a step toward Cody. "Oh really," he retorted with a smirk, looking to his companions for backup. "And when was that, last week?" The whole crew chuckled.

A glance was all it took to see that these guys weren't doing time for unpaid parking tickets. These men were well into their forties, had scarred faces, and sported jailhouse tats on their arms and necks. They were probably lifers. And who knows how they'd gotten out into all this madness.

The three of us didn't move. It would have been hard to make a break for it since we were lying on the ground.

A short white guy with a bad mullet spoke up, "Whaddya got in those packs?"

"Dirty laundry," I said, sitting up. "Wanna whiff?"

The guy with the gun took a step forward and hit my face with the butt of his gun. It didn't look like a hard hit, but it knocked me back to the ground. Clutching my nose, I saw stars for a few seconds. Something was wet. I opened my eyes and saw blood filling my hands. I couldn't tell where the blood was coming from exactly. Everything was still blurry.

"So we're going to ask you comedians one more time—what's in your packs?" the gunman said calmly. "And you've got two choices. You can crack another one of your hilarious jokes . . . " he leaned closer, "and then I'll bury the two of you and take the little lady with us. Or, you can answer politely, and we might just let you walk away."

"More like limp away," a third crewmember said. The entire crew cackled. Two of them exchanged formulaic fist bumps.

"The packs are yours," I quickly offered, not wishing any harm to come to Cody or Chelle.

"That's more like it," another man nodded.

Three men began ransacking our packs, pillaging anything they could find. They threw most of the contents onto the ground, kicking through it. They seemed to be primarily searching for food and weapons, ignoring some of our good cooking supplies like our grill and my Tupperware container of salt.

I guess these guys were too dumb to know about brining. Salt was a valuable commodity in a world without refrigeration. We often used it to brine a little bit of meat for the next day. We hadn't mastered the art yet, but it worked.

As they looted my belongings, I kept a careful eye on my khaki shorts. They quickly tossed them aside, along with my other clothes. They had no idea what they'd missed.

"I have to ask," Chelle said, "why the orange suits? No change of clothes?"

I was surprised by her question. It wasn't like Chelle to provoke people.

The gunman smiled and leaned in close to where Chelle still laid on the ground. "We seem to encounter far fewer problems when we're wearing these. It's like automatic respect." He straightened up. "Funny how that works, eh?"

Chelle pushed up on one hand. "Respect . . . or fear?"

The gunman smiled again. "Clever girl." He crouched down next to Chelle. The large man didn't have an ounce of fat on him, despite his years. His thighs were like huge trunks; his arms chiseled.

"I don't know if there's a difference between the two," he offered.

This guy might have been a prison escapee, but it was obvious he wasn't stupid. There was a reason he was in charge of this faction of fugitives. I just couldn't figure out why Chelle was pressing him.

"Oh, there definitely is a difference," Chelle rejoined. "Fear is easy to provoke. Anyone with a gun or a knife can instill fear. But respect . . . respect is a whole different neighborhood. You earn respect. You must *deserve* respect."

"Is that so?" The gunman smiled.

Chelle shrugged nonchalantly.

"Well, my little lady, I haven't had much luck earning anything in this life. And as for deserving . . . I don't really want to think about what I deserve."

"It's not too late for you," Chelle suggested.

The gunman laughed. "Ha! That's what my mom used to say." He paused, stood and stretched, then looked out over the water. "But she was wrong in the long run. I never did come around."

"Not yet," Chelle clarified.

"Ha." The gunman laughed again and then looked around at his comrades. "You seem to have a lot of faith in mankind. Don't you know that we're all inherently evil?"

"Yes," Chelle agreed, "I know that too well." Chelle stared off in the distance as her thoughts lingered for a moment.

The gunman looked at her. "Well, trust me. I'm beyond fixing."

Chelle looked up at the man with the shotgun and said firmly, "No one is beyond redemption."

He paused once again and stared into Chelle's eyes, seemingly lost in thought. I couldn't see clearly from where I was lying, but it looked like his eyes teared up a bit. And then he whispered something to himself. I think he said "Zoe."

Finally, with a shake of his head he turned back to his crew. "Let's move."

"What?" one guy asked, surprised.

The intimidating gunman shot a hard look at his men. They didn't look happy, but they weren't about to cross their formidable leader. Whatever malevolent plans he'd had for our defenseless little group had obviously changed.

"We roll. Now!" the gunman barked.

Several of the guys sighed in disagreement, shook their heads, and turned to leave. The short white guy with the mullet picked up a knife from Cody's pile of supplies and shoved it into his pocket before following the others.

The gunman leaned down next to Chelle and looked to the side as he whispered to her, "You're a special little lady."

"And you're not a lost cause," Chelle said quietly.

The gunman chuckled and shook his head once again. "Ha. There you go again." He stood up.

"Do you mind if I ask your name?" Chelle asked.

He began to walk away. "People call me Money."

Chelle called after him, "But what did your mom call you?"

Money stopped in his tracks. He turned back to look at Chelle and winked. Then he disappeared into the canopy of trees.

JOURNAL ENTRY #9

///

Something to Think About
Back to Reality . . .

• Why do you think Money didn't harm them any further?

• What's the difference between fearing someone and respecting someone?

• What did Money mean when he said, "I'm beyond fixing"?

THE BIBLE PROVIDES SOME GOOD WISDOM:

"Later, Matthew invited Jesus and his disciples to his home as dinner guests, along with many tax collectors and other disreputable sinners. But when the Pharisees saw this, they asked his disciples, 'Why does your teacher eat with such scum?'

When Jesus heard this, he said, 'Healthy people don't need a doctor—sick people do.' Then he added, 'Now go and learn the meaning of this Scripture: 'I want you to show mercy, not offer sacrifices.' For I have come to call not those who think they are righteous, but those who know they are sinners.'" (Matthew 9:10-13, NLT)

• What did Jesus mean when he said, "healthy people don't need a doctor—sick people do"?

• Is anyone beyond redemption? (See Romans 5:8.)

• Is there anyone in your life who seems "beyond redemption"? What attitude do we need to have toward these people? (See Matthew 5:44.)

SOMETHING I CAN DO THIS WEEK:

Matthew 5:44 instructs us not only to love our enemies, but also pray for them. Take a moment and pray for the person you thought of in the question above. Ask God to work in this person's life since you know he or she is not "beyond redemption." Ask God how he can use you to reach out to him or her.

THE SMOKER

Food and shelter. Those are two of the biggest necessities after water. Shelter has always come easy for us, what with all of the abandoned places around the Sacramento suburbs. But food . . . food is a daily struggle.

It probably wasn't until almost a year after The Havoc that food became scarce. During the first year, we could usually find some canned goods in an abandoned home or store. Before long, though, even the canned goods vanished. That's when we had to develop our hunting skills.

You'd think hunting was the difficult part, but it wasn't. In a world with no ovens, no stoves, and no microwaves, cooking the food was more difficult. We used some little propane grills for a while. But I guess everyone had that same idea, because propane was almost impossible to find now. So everything had to be cooked over an open fire.

That's probably why so many of us have turned to eating bugs. Bugs and fruit. Two foods that don't require any preparation. But after about five days of eating bugs, you start to crave something a little more substantial, like squirrel or geese.

It wasn't hard to shoot a bird or trap rabbits or even squirrels. Sometimes Slippery would even do the work for us. But preparing them proved to be a huge chore.

Skinning animals isn't any fun. Cabella Bill showed us how to do it. Just a couple of slices in the right place, and then pull. (Chelle puked the first time she did it.) But even after all that skinning or defeathering . . . you still need to cook it.

It took a while for us to learn how to make the perfect cooking fire. We tried doing what we'd seen in cartoons growing up: two sticks holding up a spit. But the flames usually just blackened the animal, making it super dry and crunchy—barely worth eating.

Eventually, we learned to get a bunch of good coals burning real hot. Then we set a piece of a shopping cart down as our grill, not six inches over those coals. We cooked most meat on that kind of fire, and it turned out pretty well.

But each day presented the task of building a perfect fire; hunting, skinning, and then cooking an animal. The process literally took hours. And if a large group of strays stumbled upon us, we had to evacuate, abandon our nice fire, and then build another one before we could eat again.

That is, until we met Lorin.

Lorin spent some time living in Africa as a missionary, and he learned how to build a smoker when he was there. So when Lorin came back to the States, he taught his whole family how to smoke jerky. When we stumbled across Lorin and his daughters, he offered us some jerky. Immediately, Cody and I asked, "How do you make this stuff?"

So Lorin showed us how to build a smoker and taught us how to use it.

This handy little skill has been a real lifesaver. For the year prior, we'd wasted meat more times than we could count. There'd been times when we'd actually found and killed a deer, cooked it that same evening, and then even with three of us gorging ourselves as though it was our last meal (and it easily could have been), we had plenty of meat left over.

We'd tried brining meat, but that was an art in itself. We'd cut off strips of meat, lay them out, and cover them with salt. Ideally, this was supposed to dry out the meat like smoking did.

The problems with this method were pests and the taste. Brined meat tastes terrible!

Even with brining, we'd always had a lot of meat left over whenever we shot big game. And with no refrigeration, the meat went bad.

But now whenever we kill something, especially something as big as a deer or a goat, we smoke a good portion of the meat. This provides us with enough jerky for days, which is really handy to have when we're constantly on the move.

This principle has taught us to save during times of plenty, rather than just gorging ourselves in the moment. I've said it before, and I'll say it again: You never know where your next meal is coming from. Lorin's principle of packing away some jerky has literally been a lifesaver.

JOURNAL ENTRY #10

//

Something to Think About
Back to Reality . . .

- How would you cook meat over a fire?

- How many times a day, on average, do you get something to eat (count your meals, plus all snacks)?

THE BIBLE PROVIDES SOME GOOD WISDOM:

*"The wise store up choice food and olive oil,
but fools gulp theirs down."* (Proverbs 21:20, NIV)

- What do the wise do?

- What would this piece of wisdom look like in the real world today?

SOMETHING I CAN DO THIS WEEK:

Write out a budget containing all of your income (even if it's just allowance) and all of your bills (even if you have only a few places where you spend your money). Make a plan to save a little for the future. Revisit your plan after a month and see how you did.

I PROMISE

"Nope. I'm staying right here until my parents come back."

The kid wouldn't budge. She'd been up in that tree for hours. Nothing was persuading her to come down. She'd be dead in a day or two if we left her there. It didn't seem right to leave her.

It's funny the people we encounter on the road in this crazy world: mostly adults, some teenagers like us, but rarely do we meet little kids. This little girl couldn't have been more than eight years old, and she was by herself. She said she was with her mom and dad when they happened upon a pack of strays. They got split up, and this little girl climbed a tree unnoticed as the strays chased after her parents.

Cody happened to hear her rustling in the branches above us when we walked by, and we spent the next hour trying to talk her into coming down so we could take her somewhere safe.

Chelle decided to give it a try.

"Where do you think your parents are now?" That's a funny question, if you think about it. This girl's parents were probably dead. Who cares where she *thought* her parents were?

"They're probably at home. We always meet at home if we get split up."

"Where's home?" Chelle asked. "Is it close?"

"It's by the Big Buy."

Big Buy was the best place to get electronics before The Havoc. There was a huge one in the Birdcage outdoor shopping area not five minutes from where we used to live. Years ago, my dad and I stood in line in outside that store until midnight when Nintendo's new *Hologram Mario* game came out. We knew the store well.

"Is it a house by the Big Buy?" Chelle asked.

"Nope." The little girl said. "It's an apartment. I can see the Big Buy from our front window."

"I know exactly where that is," I told Chelle.

Chelle looked back up at the little girl. "We know where that is. Let us take you there."

The little girl thought about it for a moment. "I can't."

"Why not?"

"I'm not supposed to go anywhere with strangers."

We all sighed.

Cody leaned in close, "This isn't getting us anywhere. It's getting late."

"I know," Chelle whispered. "But we can't just leave her here. You know she won't make it if we do."

"That's her problem," Cody said.

Chelle shot Cody a hard look and then looked back up at the girl.

"My name is Chelle. What's yours?"

The little girl was quiet.

"If you tell me your name, maybe I can help you."

After a long pause, she finally said, "What's your dog's name?"

"Slippery. What's your name?"

Silence.

Chelle whispered to us, "Play along." She looked back up at the little girl and said, "Okay. I guess we'll be leaving now." Chelle put on her pack. We followed her cue. "Have a good night's sleep up in that tree. Watch out for the strays."

"The strays?" the little girl asked.

"Yeah. The dead people walking around."

"Oh. The eaters."

That's one thing we noticed in this crazy world. Everyone had different names for the strays. No one knew what to call them. We'd heard a lot of terms: Freaks, John Does, Squirlies... even heard a couple people use the word zombie.

The three of us began walking away.

When we were about 30 yards from her tree, the little girl shouted, "Don't go!"

Chelle stopped and said, "I thought you didn't want our help. We're strangers."

The little girl was silent again.

Chelle walked back under the tree. "Okay. I have an idea. Big Buy isn't but three miles from here. How about we go to your house and . . . "

"My apartment," the little girl said.

"Yes . . . I mean your apartment. How about we go get your parents at your apartment and bring them back here."

The little girl thought for a moment. "You'd do that?"

Chelle made eye contact with me and Cody. "Yes, we'd do that."

"Promise?"

Chelle looked at us, wanting our approval. I nodded yes. Cody sighed and nodded a frustrated yes.

"Yes. We promise," Chelle said. "Now, do you know your address?"

"No."

"Nice," Cody said under his breath.

Chelle looked like she was going to clock Cody in the jaw. I'd never seen that look before. And apparently Cody hadn't either, because he quickly looked down at his feet.

"Describe it to us," Chelle said. "You said it's an apartment facing Big Buy. What else?"

The little girl thought for a moment. "It has a brown door . . . and a hedgehog."

"A hedgehog?" Chelle looked confused.

"Yeah. Spikey. You wipe your feet on him."

"Is Spikey out front?"

"Yep. He guards our door."

We finally convinced the girl that we would get her parents and bring them back to get her. We hid our packs in some brush near the tree, and set out on foot. The sun was getting low, so we stepped up our pace.

After carefully crossing Sunrise Boulevard, we slipped over to the Birdcage shopping area. It was one of the first outdoor malls. Half of it had burned down; the other half was looted within the first few weeks of The Havoc. The Big Buy was around the back.

As we cautiously rounded the corner, we saw a discouraging sight. The Big Buy parking lot was overrun with strays. A huge pack of them were attacking something in the middle of the parking lot, and others wandered the streets between the Big Buy and the nearby apartments.

We crouched down low behind a tipped-over truck in the parking lot.

"There are hundreds of 'em," Cody said quietly, verbalizing what we were all thinking.

Chelle pointed to a group of apartments clearly in sight of the Big Buy. Strays were walking around on the front lawn of the apartments. "That must be where she lives."

We sat in silence, realizing we'd bitten off way more than we could chew.

"Chelle?" I finally asked. "You realize there's no way we can get to that apartment."

Chelle just stood there, looking at the chaotic scene.

"Chelle!" I touched her arm.

She jerked her arm away and said angrily, "I know! I know! But we can't just leave. We've gotta do this."

"What do you mean, '*We've* gotta do this'?" Cody asked. "We *can't* do it."

Chelle looked at us. "It doesn't matter if we can't. We will try to do it because we said we would."

"Yeah, but we didn't know . . . "

"Does it matter?" Chelle barked, looking more serious than I'd ever seen her. "We said we would. Case closed. Now, will one of you guys please figure out a plan?"

We sat in silence as we looked out across the overrun parking lot. As I looked, I began trying to figure out ways to reason with Chelle.

Then Cody spoke up. "I got it."

"What?" we asked in unison.

"We just need a distraction." Cody said, "I'll handle that. You get to the apartment." He reached out and clasped hands with me and looked into my eyes. "I'll see you back at the place where we camped last night." He looked at Slippery, "You stay here, boy." And before I could utter a word of disagreement, he disappeared around the back of a sporting goods store.

About a minute later, we heard echoing laughter from the distance. We looked toward the street between the Big Buy and the apartments. Cody was walking out in the open and laughing hysterically. And then he started singing.

*"I know, you know, that I'm not telling the truth
I know, you know they just don't have any proof . . . "*

"What's he singing?" Chelle asked.

I couldn't laugh because I was too terrified for my brother's safety. "It's the theme song to that old show, *Psych*."

*"Embrace the deception, learn how to bend
Your worst inhibitions tend to psych you out in the end.*

*"I know, you know
I know, you know . . . "*

One by one, strays started sprinting toward Cody. Instead of turning around, Cody ran straight into the parking lot and looped through a slower group of them. Then he turned back toward where he'd come from and poured on the speed like only Cody could.

Sure enough, the parking lot emptied. They took off after Cody like greyhounds chasing the mechanical rabbit. Except this rabbit was still singing, and singing incredibly out of tune.

*"In between the lines there's a lot of obscurity
I'm not inclined to resign to maturity . . . "*

He disappeared around the corner with all of the strays on his six.

Not two minutes later, Chelle and I were standing on the front porch of the little girl's apartment, complete with a brown door and a spikey hedgehog brush for cleaning off your dirty shoes. Slippery sniffed the hedgehog.

"Let me handle this," Chelle said. She began pounding on the door and yelling, "We found your daughter! She needs you!"

Inside, we heard a muffled voice yell, "Candice, no!"

A woman frantically opened the door. "Where? Where's my daughter?"

The man came running up behind her with a shotgun in his hands. We slowly raised our arms in the air, and Chelle talked quickly, "We found your daughter over by the footbridge in River Bend Park. She's up in a tree, and she won't come down because we're strangers. We told her we'd go get you."

The woman smiled through her tears. "Thank God!"

The man lowered his shotgun and came with us.

Three hours later, we sat around our camp reflecting on the day. Cody told us about the obstacle course he'd taken the strays through before finally losing them, and we told him about the little girl's parents. Her name was Sidney, stubborn little thing. Maybe that's why she's still alive.

I finally told Chelle, "You did the right thing back there. I'm embarrassed to admit it, but I don't know if I would have done that."

Chelle stirred the fire with a stick. The fire was hot. And a hot fire gives off very little smoke. Finally she looked up at us and said, "I told her I would." And that's all she said for the rest of the night.

JOURNAL ENTRY #11

///

Something to Think About
Back to Reality . . .

• What would you have done in this situation?

• Why was Chelle so adamant about getting to those apartments?

• When Cody and Chris were having doubts about keeping their word to the little girl, Chelle acted as a moral compass. She insisted, "We said we would. Case closed." What did she mean?

THE BIBLE PROVIDES SOME GOOD WISDOM:

In Psalm 15, David describes people who "do what is right." He lists numerous characteristics, including those who "keep their promises even when it hurts" (Psalm 15:4, NLT).

• What does it mean to keep a promise, even when it hurts?

• Describe a time you made a promise that was pretty tough to keep. Why was it so tough? Is it okay for us to break our word when things get difficult? Explain.

• Why is it important to God that we keep our word?

SOMETHING I CAN DO THIS WEEK:

Read Psalm 15 this week, then pray and ask God to help you become a person who seeks to do what is right . . . even when it hurts.

THE ISLAND

A world where the dead roam the earth is a *restless* world. I mean that in the truest sense of the word restless. It's hard to *rest* in a world where you need to be on guard at any given moment, awake or asleep.

That's probably why we were so ecstatic to discover the island.

Strays don't do well in a current. We learned that early on while fishing in the North Fork American River. A stray would take a step or two into the water, become disoriented and unstable in the current, and stumble back to shore.

Needless to say, we spend lots of time in the water now, when the weather permits. It's nice to have a neutral zone, of sorts, a place where we know strays won't sneak up on us.

It was during one of the first times when I was splashing around with Cody and Chelle that I remembered the island. I scolded myself for not thinking of it sooner, but it had only dawned on me in that instant.

Cody was also to blame for forgetting about it, because he'd been to the island with me several times. Our next-door neighbor Matt had shown it to us in when I was in sixth grade. It was in the middle of Lake Natoma, just east of the Nimbus Dam in Fair Oaks. The lake used to be a section of the American River before the dams were built, and it still flows like a river, growing wider just before the dam. They named the body of water Lake Natoma, and it grew to be one of the more popular recreation areas in the Sacramento region.

The island, however, was upstream from there. Only kayakers knew about it because it was too far from the shore for most swimmers to reach. The island was small—probably about a quarter of an acre, so not much bigger than the typical property of suburban track home in California. It was covered with rocks and pine trees, and it was home to a few wild geese. Before The Havoc, kayakers would sometimes stop to rest and explore the island. It took just a couple of minutes to explore the tiny landmass in its entirety.

Cody and I had first learned of it when Matt took us there in his small raft. We called it our "secret island." Out of all the times we were on that island as kids, we encountered another person just once. Two longhaired guys, covered with tats, were leaning back against their beached canoe and smoking something with a peculiar odor. We didn't stick around to discover what they were smoking.

So Cody, Chelle, Slippery, and I ventured up to Lake Natoma one morning to check out the island and see if anyone else had the same idea. We were all in pretty good shape, so we could have swum it. But we didn't want to leave our packs on the shore. We had quite a bit of jerky, some apples, sleeping bags, and some pretty nice cooking supplies. So we walked the shores westbound toward the old Sacramento State Aquatic Center. They used to rent out fishing boats, kayaks; you name it.

By noon, we'd hopped the fence and discovered a row of tandem kayaks chained together. Cody pulled the bolt cutters out of his pack (probably one of the handiest tools we carry with us) and snipped the lock. Within 30 minutes, we were paddling two kayaks up Lake Natoma. Chelle and I were in one boat; Cody and Slippery were in the other one.

Our small vessels glided easily across the water, and we enjoyed the cool air coming off the surface of the lake. As we approached the island, some geese swam out to greet us—a good sign. The small land mass looked empty from a distance. But we wanted to be sure it was uninhabited. So we circled the island from about 100 feet out, and then slowly spiraled in, eventually beaching our vessels in the soft dirt.

A quick exploration of the island revealed it to be as empty as we'd hoped. The dirt was soft, and the shade was plentiful. By nightfall we had a nice fire going, and a goose was cooking on the grill.

That was probably one of the best night's sleep I'd had in years, simply because I knew that nothing dead could possibly creep up on us in the middle of the night.

For the next week, we stayed on the island, laughing, playing in the water, and going on short kayak rides. It was an amazing week of rest. It was sort of like a vacation.

The island wasn't a fortress, by any means. We always wondered it we'd find a safe place like that—a place with sturdy walls but also lots of survivors. There was safety in numbers. But most of the humans we'd encountered seemed to be as alone in this new world as we were.

After the goose meat ran out and the jerky was long gone, it was time to move on. But we left the island feeling truly rested. We've returned to the island numerous times since then. It's undeniably our favorite place to rest.

It's important to find a place where you can truly relax—even if the dead are walking the earth. After all, everyone needs a break.

JOURNAL ENTRY #12

///

Something to Think About
Back to Reality . . .

• The island was a place where they could relax and let down their guard. Where do you go to do that?

THE BIBLE PROVIDES SOME GOOD WISDOM:

"Six days you shall labor, but on the seventh day you shall rest; even during the plowing season and harvest you must rest." (Exodus 34:21, NIV)

• Why do you think God tells his people to rest?

• God specifically mentions that "even during the plowing season and harvest you must rest." The planting and harvesting seasons are the busiest times for farmers. Do God's people rest during their busy times? Why or why not?

• What does rest look like in your world?

SOMETHING YOU CAN DO THIS WEEK:

Talk with your parents about what you learned.

And then try resting this Sunday. Get all of your homework and chores done by Saturday night so you can truly relax on Sunday.

WHILE THEY SLEEP

Every time we think we finally understand these stupid creatures, they do something to surprise us.

Luckily, this surprise was actually helpful.

Our supply of jerky was nearly gone, so we were hunting just off the American River bike trail. We frequently encountered small game near this trail, so we'd decided we'd try to find something that we could cook in the outdoor fireplace we'd discovered in the backyard of an abandoned house in Fair Oaks.

That morning, we'd left Slippery back at the house, crossed the footbridge to the bike trail, and began moving west.

By late afternoon we hadn't encountered anything—not even a squirrel. So we headed back to the house, keeping our eyes on the sun.

We don't like being out after dark if we don't have to be. Our eyes and ears had proven to be our best senses for anticipating danger. But darkness reduces that ability by half.

As the sun slowly disappeared below the tree line, we heard a group of people wandering up the trail. The three of us didn't take any chances. We ducked behind the river embankment, well hidden by a clump of Manzanita bushes.

The group turned out to be a bunch of big dudes wearing black leather. We'd never seen such a gathering of large, bulky men before. The smallest looked to be about the size of Money (that Folsom prisoner we'd encountered on the riverbank months prior). He was probably 6'2" and weighed at least 250. Each man carried a bat or a club, and they looked like they knew how to use them.

Of all the places they could have stopped, they chose to sit under a tree not 30 yards from where we were crouched. After just five minutes of eavesdropping on their conversations, we were glad we'd stayed hidden.

An hour later, the group decided to set up camp and stay the night. We were now trapped. There were only two ways to leave our current position: the path in front of this group of barbarians, or the river.

As the sun dipped out of sight, we opted to slip into the river, gear and all. We each took off our shoes and socks and held them above the water (wet, squeaky shoes are a death sentence in this world), and then we submerged our bodies into the biting cold water and quietly waded under the curtain of darkness.

About a half-mile upstream, we emerged from the water and did our best to wring out our clothes before pulling on our dry shoes and socks. Luckily, we'd left most of our supplies hidden back at the house. Now we carried just a bow and arrows, a machete, and some canteens we used for drinking water.

Shivering in the Delta breeze, we made our way back to the bridge. The moon wasn't up yet, and dark clouds covered the stars. It was almost impossible to navigate through the black night. But we soon found the bridge and slowly began walking to the north side of the river.

With the wind at our backs, we stepped cautiously and kept completely silent, not knowing what lurked ahead. About 20 yards onto the bridge, we stopped. I grabbed Cody's and Chelle's arms and made a slight sniffing sound.

I couldn't see their faces in the darkness, but I know they

smelled it too: the unbearable odor of a stray—maybe even multiple strays. It was foul.

The breeze died for a moment, and it smelled like we were waist-deep in sewage. I started to say something but hesitated. I could hear someone breathing . . . and it wasn't Cody or Chelle.

The three of us froze. We didn't move for moments that seemed to stretch into hours. But then the clouds moved, and a few stars began to peek through. As our eyes adjusted to the darkness, we were horrified by what we saw.

We were standing on a bridge blanketed with sleeping strays. Bodies lay everywhere across the bridge. I'd never seen such a gathering before, and never had so many of them been sleeping.

It was a bizarre experience. Occasionally we'd come across sleeping strays inside the stores we were searching. And they'd always become quite hostile when we startled them. But never had we seen so many of them asleep like this.

As peaceful as they seemed, I didn't want to be here if something startled them. So I signaled to Cody and Chelle, and we began sneaking our way through the maze of bodies, stepping over them, around them, pretty much anyplace we could find footing.

The north side of the bridge was almost wall-to-wall bodies. I began to doubt my decision to press on. Perhaps we should have turned back when we first discovered the danger. It would have added an hour or two—and a swim—to our trip, but anything was better than this!

Some strays snored, while others just breathed heavily. The stench was unbearable now. I held back the urge to retch;

although I don't know what I would have vomited because my stomach was completely empty. I caught a glimpse of Chelle's face as she looked down at all the bodies. She was terrified. She looked as if she were going to cry.

I gently placed my hand on her arm and made eye contact with her. I mouthed, "It's okay," and then smiled. I motioned for her to keep her eyes locked on mine.

With 10 feet more to go, Cody's foot got caught on the boot of a stray. He tripped and fell, making a huge *thud!* As his body hit the wooden planks of the bridge. My mom would have described it as a noise that would "wake the dead."

We all froze.

Two strays stirred slightly but continued sleeping. Thank goodness Mom was wrong!

Apparently their senses aren't very acute. Cody's fall surely would have woken any human sleeping nearby. Maybe that's why their balance is so poor and they can't walk in rivers. Maybe their ears and their equilibrium are inept.

We decided not to stick around to find out.

Cody quietly returned to his feet, and we finished navigating the labyrinth of slumbering corpses. Eventually, our feet found pavement on the other side of the bridge. And then our walk became a run—ultimately an all-out sprint.

We didn't stop running until we'd safely climbed into the backyard of the house where we were staying. Slippery greeted us with a friendly bark and a wagging tail.

Chelle sighed. "I really thought we were done. I mean it. I thought that was it."

I nodded between gasps. "I was scared too."

"I think we just made it through the darkest valley," Chelle quoted from Psalm 23. We'd read it the night before.

Cody chuckled, "Yeah, except I was definitely afraid."

"I've never seen them sleep like that," I said, trying to figure out what we'd just experienced.

"And they barely stirred when Cody fell," Chelle added. "Heavy sleepers."

"This is a good thing," Cody said. "That means they actually need sleep . . . or at least they enjoy it or something. We can totally use this to our advantage!"

With adrenaline still pulsating through our veins, the three of us went into the house and got ready for bed. We hadn't eaten in more than 24 hours, but none of us cared. We hadn't been eaten either. Thank God for that.

We slipped into our sleeping bags; our stomachs were well past growling. We'd wait and eat our last bit of jerky the next morning, and maybe we'd even find some fruit. We'd gone longer between meals.

At least we were still alive . . . and a little smarter too.

JOURNAL ENTRY #13

///

Something to Think About
Back to Reality . . .

• Describe a time when you were the most frightened you've ever been. How did you respond?

THE BIBLE PROVIDES SOME GOOD WISDOM:

"Even when I walk
through the darkest valley,
I will not be afraid,
for you are close beside me . . ." (Psalm 23:4, NLT)

• Why does the author of this psalm write that he "will not be afraid"?

• Describe why it's comforting to remember that God is our Shepherd.

• If God knows what's best for us and is with us through the darkest times, does that mean God won't allow us to be hurt?

Psalm 23 ends with this:

"Surely your goodness and unfailing love will pursue me
all the days of my life,
and I will live in the house of the LORD
forever." (Psalm 23:6, NLT)

• What will pursue us? What does this look like?

• In the midst of our fears in this temporary world, how comforting is God's promise that those who trust him will receive a new life in a new world for all eternity?

SOMETHING I CAN DO THIS WEEK:

Try reading Psalm 23 and a few other psalms, observing
how King David and some of the other authors rely on God's
strength through good times and bad. Notice their eternal focus.
God provides comfort in the temporary because we have hope
in him in the eternal.

THE SPRING

Talk to anyone who's survived in the wild, and they'll tell you about the three majors: water, food, and shelter—usually in that order.

Water wasn't a problem at first. When The Havoc first started, houses still had running water. That lasted for months. If we were thirsty, we could always find a faucet in any house or building.

Then the city's water supply went bad.

Water wasn't too hard to find, though. Most abandoned stores had cases of bottled water lying around. Cody and I always carried a few bottles with us in our packs. And during that first year, it was rare to be beyond reach of a new supply.

Eventually even the bottled water became impossible to find. When people realized this, the reverse-osmosis filters were the first to disappear off the store shelves. Fresh water quickly became priority number one. And to a group of teenagers who knew nothing about water purification, this was a little scary.

When he was in middle school, Cody went to a backpacking camp with a friend. One of the things they learned that week was how to find fresh water sources. They went backpacking in the Sierra Mountains where there were plenty of small creeks and rivers to choose from. And Cody remembered how the leader had said it was best to find moving water that ran downhill—so many feet of elevation per feet of distance. Cody, of course, couldn't remember what that ratio was. But the leader had also said it's safer to either boil water or use water purification tablets, because the water in rivers and streams might contain microscopic organisms like giardia. One time our friend Scott got sick because of those. Not a pretty sight.

Boiling water isn't hard to do, but it's a discipline. Think about it: Every night once we find a safe place to camp, the first thing we have to do is make a fire, boil a couple of gallons of water, let it cool, and then pour it into our canteens for the next day. Two gallons was usually the perfect amount because each person needs to drink about two quarts of water a day. (We could live on less than that if we ate a lot of fruit, which has water in it. But we needed to drink more water during the summer months when it was really hot.)

The problem was those nights when we were in hiding and couldn't build a fire. An occasional day without water quickly convinced us that we needed to do something in addition to the boiling method for water our purification.

A quick raid of a sports supply store yielded a couple of canteens and a nice supply of water purification tablets. These were incredibly handy for those nights without fires or those days when we were constantly on the move. But eventually, the purification tablets ran out. That's when we tried bleach.

Our friend Taylor told us that bleach would purify water if you used the proper mixture. He told us to start with eight drops of bleach per gallon of water, shake it, and then wait 20 minutes. He said the water should have a slight chlorine odor. If it doesn't, then the bleach might have been used up while killing all the organisms in the water. That means you need more bleach. So add eight more drops and wait again. We've never used more than a double dose. Worse case, it tasted like a swimming pool.

The constant chore of boiling and purifying water is monotonous. That's probably why we were so happy to find a spring last May. It was during one of our expeditions in Northern California. We'd gone up there to explore the farmlands west of Mount Lassen, near Redding. But we came across an abandoned national park called Shasta Spring.

So we followed the river until it disappeared under a rock in the side of the mountain. For about five minutes, Cody and I debated whether or not the water was fresh enough to drink. Slippery didn't hesitate. He waded right in and started lapping it up.

"See!" Cody declared. "Slippery likes it."

The fact was, neither of us knew whether microorganisms lived in underground springs. So Cody finally took his canteen and held it under the running water.

When his hand submerged in the water, he scrunched up his nose and looked at me. "It's cold."

He pulled out his canteen and guzzled the cool, clear water.

"Ah!" he smiled. "Wow! That's the best water I've tasted in a year!"

Call me impulsive, but I didn't wait to see if he'd get sick. His taste test was good enough for me. I dumped out the remaining quart of last night's boiled water from my canteen and filled it with the fresh, cold spring water coming from who-knows-where underneath the mountain.

I brought the canteen to my lips and let the icy water trickle down my throat. Cody was right. It tasted amazing. I didn't remember water tasting so good.

Cody and I drank like two hobbits at a pub.

Time passed and nothing happened. We didn't throw up (or worse . . . the other end). Instead, we just filled our bellies and sprawled in the cool grass by the edge of the spring.

We found an abandoned cabin nearby and stayed there for a

few months. We were definitely spoiled by the convenient fresh water source. As winter approached, we headed south again to avoid the cold weather. But we knew we'd be back, and the next time we'd bring along more empty containers.

Drinking water isn't easy to come by, and it's a daily task to replenish it. We learned that if you find a spring, cherish it. It's a life source we no longer take for granted.

JOURNAL ENTRY #14

//

Something to Think About
Back to Reality . . .

• What would you do if the water in your city were contaminated?

• Why did Chris used the word *cherish* to express how much he valued water? What does that word mean?

• Have you ever cherished something? Explain.

THE BIBLE PROVIDES SOME GOOD WISDOM:

"Jesus answered, 'Everyone who drinks this water will be thirsty again, but whoever drinks the water I give them will never thirst. Indeed, the water I give them will become in them a spring of water welling up to eternal life.'" (John 4:13-14, NIV)

• In this passage of Scripture, Jesus is trying to help us understand that he has something for us that will fill us up forever. If we drink his water, we will never be thirsty again. What do you think this means? What will happen to those who drink the water Jesus gives them?

Note: Just like we need food and water to survive, Jesus is explaining that we need his "living water" to survive spiritually. We need to be connected to him, drawing nourishment and strength from him.

• What are some ways we can connect to Jesus and draw strength from him?

SOMETHING I CAN DO THIS WEEK:

Plan a specific time to do one of the things you just wrote about for the last question. Add a reminder on your phone or calendar, if that will help.

For further reading: Later in this book of John, Jesus uses another analogy, saying, "I am the vine; you are the branches" (John 15:5). He's reminding us of how important it is to stay connected to him, and the consequences of disconnecting from him. (See John 15:1-11.)

DON'T MISTAKE YOUR BROTHER FOR A STRAY

Cody and I are inseparable. We look out for each other, we think alike, and we actually get along most of the time—in spite of the fact that we're brothers.

That's why I'm so glad I didn't kill him yesterday.

It started when Cody went hunting. Cody is the better shot with a bow and arrow, and I was tending the fire. Day quickly turned to night, and Cody wasn't back yet.

We don't like splitting up, but survival calls for it at times. Sometimes we don't have enough time to hunt, make a fire, boil water, establish a stray warning string around the perimeter, and do all of the other necessary tasks. So one of us hunts while the other one sets up camp.

Numerous times one of us has come across a pack of strays or worse—a group of human scavengers. And then we have to stay in hiding until the coast is clear, separated from our little group. But over the last four years, we've learned to predict the strays' moves. Humans are never predictable. They're innately self-seeking and few of them are trustworthy.

We rarely engage with other survivors we meet on the road. Staying put usually proves wise, as we've seen what many of these groups will do when they encounter other survivors. (I have a scar on my nose to prove it.) So we've learned it's best to stay hidden and sneak away once they leave the area or go to sleep.

Last night, Cody still wasn't back, and it was long after the sun had dropped below the horizon. That usually meant trouble. Long ago we agreed that if we hadn't found what we were looking for by sunset, we'd rejoin the group within our best guess of an hour—and it was truly a guess since we couldn't look at the time on our cell phones anymore. If we weren't back in an hour, the base camp group was to kill the fire, stay put, and be on the lookout for danger.

When Cody didn't show up, Chelle and I began packing up the camp. Luckily, I'd already boiled the water, but I was still a little perturbed about having to put out my nice coals. They would have been perfect for roasting whatever game Cody had caught.

But the focus of my worries wasn't my stomach right then. I was more concerned about my brother. Even Slippery seemed anxious. He'd perched on a rock and was looking off in the direction where Cody had walked hours before. I should have sent the dog went with him.

When everything but the stray tripwire was packed, Chelle and I climbed an oak tree that provided a good amount of distance from the ground, excellent nighttime camouflage, and two escape routes: one huge branch hanging over the land, and another extending over the river. Slippery laid by a bush near the foot of the tree.

We'd just gotten comfortable—as comfortable as you can be in a tree—when we heard the bells of our tripwire jingle. I wrapped my fingers tighter around the handle of my machete.

A dark figure crawled though the brush, creeping toward our camp. Slippery let out a low growl.

This can't be Cody, I thought. Cody wouldn't have tripped on our warning string, and Cody would have made his dove coo noise if he knew we were nearby. Cody had to know this was our camp . . . didn't he?

The dark figure slowly stood and walked closer to where our fire once burned. He was now 10 feet away from the tree and getting closer.

I slowly raised the machete, ready to drop on top of the individual if I felt we were in any danger. And the hairs on the back of my neck were telling me we were in danger.

The figure stopped right below me and raised his hands to his mouth. The next sound I heard was a huge relief.

A dove's coo.

I returned the coo from above. Cody startled and pulled back an arrow in his bow. "Chris?" he hissed.

"You're late," I quickly retorted. "Now put that bow down before you accidentally shoot me."

Chelle and I jumped down from the tree and threw our arms around him. Slippery greeted him as well with his tail wagging. I squeezed Cody tightly—part love and part frustration.

"What happened? Why didn't you warn us that it was you?" I asked, finally seeing his eyes in the moonlight.

"I caught a beaver—a nice big one. But then I ran into a pack of strays on the way back. I was having trouble shaking them, so I had to ditch the beaver in order to occupy them while I slipped away."

"So much for dinner," I interjected.

"I know, right?" Cody said quickly. "I got turned around, and it took me quite a while to get back to you. And I didn't even feel or hear the tripwire."

"You're welcome," Chelle said proudly. "That's the point, right?"

"I'm just glad you're safe!" I said.

"Me too," Chelle said.

"Me too!" Cody agreed. He turned to me. "Next time, you go hunting, and I'll stay behind with the pretty girl!"

JOURNAL ENTRY #15

///

Something to Think About
Back to Reality . . .

• What do you like about their plan to never be separated fore more than an hour after sunset?

• Have you ever mistaken a friend or family member for a stranger? When did you finally know it was really him or her?

THE BIBLE PROVIDES SOME GOOD WISDOM:

"My sheep listen to my voice; I know them, and they follow me." (John 10:27, NIV)

• In John, chapter 10, Jesus tells the people, "I am the good shepherd; I know my sheep and my sheep know me" (v. 14). He goes on to say in verse 27, "My sheep listen to my voice." How do you think Jesus' followers (his sheep) listen to his voice?

• How do we get to know Jesus better so we can hear his voice?

• In verse 27, what does Jesus say his sheep do once they listen to his voice?

SOMETHING I CAN DO THIS WEEK:

Make a specific plan to get to know Jesus better this week by tuning in to his voice. You can plan a time to read the Bible or maybe listen to a Christian message or podcast. Listen for God's voice, the truth he is telling you through his Word.

CLIMBING

When I was a kid, I was terrified of bears.

We'd go camping in Yosemite, which is full of bears. Friendly? Sure. But tell that to an eight-year-old.

I remember my cousin Billy telling me, "If a bear wants to kill you, you're gonna die." All the cousins would gather around him as he shared his great wisdom. (Billy was the oldest.) "If you run, the bear will catch you. They can run 35 miles an hour through the woods. If you try to shoot it, it won't do any good. A bullet will just bounce right off his skull. If you try to climb a tree, he'll just climb up after you and get you. Bears are excellent climbers."

Who knows how much Billy really knew about bears? It didn't matter. He had all of us convinced. If we saw a bear, we knew we were dead!

As I grew older, I reflected on Billy's logic. Bears will climb up after you? Really? A 600-pound bear is going to climb as high as a 120-pound kid?

Maybe that's why Cody, Chelle, and I scurried up a tree the first time a pack of strays chased us. We must have figured they can't climb. Either that, or we were just tired of running.

Luckily, we were right. The first time we tried climbing, we didn't have a choice. We'd salvaged some cooking supplies from a diner in downtown Sacramento and headed toward the Sacramento River. We ended up navigating the campus of California State University; and in our haste to get to the river, we rounded a corner too fast.

A huge pack of strays, probably 100 of them, were gathered around something in the middle of the grassy quad. We never saw what it was because a handful of strays at the edge of the group noticed us looking at them and headed straight for us.

These strays weren't sluggish. We had 70 yards on them, but they were in an all-out sprint, and they seemed to be closing the distance fast. This was in the days before we had Slippery. And that was too bad because the little rascal was good at being a distraction and playing decoy.

We sprinted past a couple of administration buildings, quickly trying the doors and finding nothing unlocked. That pause costed us another 20 yards, so I yelled to Cody and Chelle, "The trees!"

Cody was the fastest. He always had been. The coach at the high school had come out to several of his middle school track meets just to see the kid who ran an 800 in less than two minutes. Cody even broke three school records. Unfortunately, the world fell to pieces before Cody got to run as a freshman. But now his speed served a much greater purpose—saving lives.

Cody got to the tree first and easily shimmied up the first few branches, just out of reach. He perched on a branch, pulled out his bow and arrow, aimed it just over our heads, and *ffffffffft*! An arrow flew past us, hitting the fastest stray right in the left eye socket.

Once that stray went down, about a dozen others pounced on him like a pack of dingoes.

We used every second Cody had just bought for us. I gave Chelle a quick boost, making sure she was clear before I scrambled up after her. More strays came at us full speed. Cody dropped two more of them, but within seconds a crowd had arrived. One reached up and touched my leg. Luckily, it couldn't get a good grip. I shook it free and ascended higher into the huge elm.

When the rest of the crowd of strays arrived, they swarmed under the tree like a pack of wild dogs. Some reached up toward the branches and grabbed at them, but they didn't seem to know what to do. None of them tried lifting themselves up; they just kept grasping at the branches and staring up at us. By this time we were 50 feet in the air, probably further than I ever would have felt comfortable climbing had there not been 100 ravenous creatures lurking below.

After we caught our breath, we realized . . . now what?

We had been "treed."

We tried our best to get comfortable. We had no other choice but to wait it out and hope the strays would give up on us.

Three hours later, the crowd had dwindled down to about a dozen. A nearby squirrel caught the attention of a few of them, and the others just wandered off.

We learned quite a bit about strays that day. We were a little premature in our deduction that they couldn't climb. One stray chased a squirrel to a nearby pine tree with low branches. As the squirrel ascended, so did the stray—rather quickly, actually—and it seemed to navigate the branches pretty easily too. The difference was that the low pine branches had provided some natural steps for the stray to climb. The strays at the base of our tree didn't seem to know where to begin.

That squirrel might have saved our lives. When it went up into the pine, not 30 yards away from us, it then jumped onto a phone line and scurried over to the roof of a nearby building. The stray then attempted to reach out for the cable, but it missed and fell, pinballing down the pine branches and landing flat on its back at the base of the tree. That fall would have killed any human . . . but this one was already dead. Needless to say, the stray got up and hobbled about three feet before a group of 10 other strays attacked it, feasting on him in the shade of the pine.

Cody didn't even notice what happened to the stray because he was intently watching the squirrel. "Look," he said, pointing as the squirrel ran along the roof and eventually hopped out of sight. Cody's eyes followed the phone line back to our tree. Then he started climbing higher. "Watch this."

"Cody, wait." I didn't think this was a good idea.

"Don't worry," Cody said with confidence. "I'll test my weight before I go."

Cody climbed another 10 feet and grabbed ahold of the thick cable. He easily lifted his body weight onto it and hung there for a while, his feet hanging freely above the branches where he'd just been standing. "See? It totally supports me. I'm going for it."

Chelle and I both looked down toward the base of the tree, hoping to see some other possible escape route. A dozen strays still surrounded the trunk, looking up and hoping a meal would drop down to them any minute.

When I looked back up, Cody had already begun moving. He'd wrapped his legs around the wire and was scooting across like a koala, but horizontally. He actually covered the distance in no time, and then dropped less than 10 feet onto the roof. Several strays on the ground had tracked Cody's progress and were now watching the roof.

Cody yelled, "Meet me at the pizza place! I'll be there later tonight!"

And before we could argue with him, he disappeared out of sight. Thirty seconds later, Cody reappeared around the corner of the building, 120 yards away from the strays below us.

He shouted, "Hey, dirtbags! Come and get it!" And the strays took off after him—every single one of them!

Cody ran like a gazelle.

Chelle and I navigated our way down the tree and crept away unnoticed.

Later that night, we silently slipped through the back door of the pizza place. Cody was already inside, crouched on top of a heating unit in the ceiling. "It's about time!"

Five minutes later we exchanged hugs.

"Good thing strays can't climb, eh?" Cody said assuredly.

"Definitely," I agreed.

JOURNAL ENTRY #16

//

Something to Think About
Back to Reality . . .

• Describe a time when you got yourself stuck or trapped. How did you finally get free?

• What are some situations from which you need to escape?

• What are some tempting/sinful situations that can "tree" you?

THE BIBLE PROVIDES SOME GOOD WISDOM:

"If you think you are standing strong, be careful not to fall. The temptations in your life are no different from what others experience. And God is faithful. He will not allow the temptation to be more than you can stand. When you are tempted, he will show you a way out so that you can endure." (1 Corinthians 10:12-13, NLT)

• What's comforting about this verse?

• When you're tempted, what does God provide?

• What is the "way out" of the tempting/sinful situation you mentioned above?

SOMETHING I CAN DO THIS WEEK:

Write out a game plan to avoid and escape tempting/sinful situations that can "tree" you. Include these three elements:
a. How can I steer clear of this temptation?
b. How can I use God's "way out" when this temptation sneaks up on me?
c. Who can I call or text to help me stand strong?

JOY RIDE

If you were to ask any living human today where they allocate most of their time, they would undoubtedly tell you that it's scouting for shelter and supplies.

In the first few years, our searches focused on food and water. Canned food and water were still available then; but by year three, most of the food was spoiled. So our reconnaissance runs were fixated on finding weapons, tarps, tools . . . and we were always on the lookout for safe neighborhoods to live in—ones that hadn't been destroyed by the fires.

Now during the last year, our searches have expanded beyond much of the Sacramento area. This means long journeys, usually done on foot. It was on one of these journeys that we learned a little more about Chelle's past.

The journey began when we woke up one morning in a quiet Roseville home. Roseville was a nice suburb northeast of Sacramento. It was nestled right next to Granite Bay, which used to be one of the wealthiest areas for hundreds of miles. Our plans were to head east up Highway 80.

After eating an apple for breakfast, I told everyone to pack up. "It's time to hit the road. We've got a long walk."

And that's when Chelle said it: "Let's drive."

Her statement caught us off guard. Sure, we'd found quite a few abandoned cars during those first few years, and we'd used them on our scouting expeditions. But gas was hard to come by now. The fuel left in most of the vehicles' tanks was too old, moisture and rust had built up, and the computer systems and fuel injectors of most cars were way too sensitive to burn this polluted gas.

So I tried to gently remind her of this fact, "Drive? What about gas?"

Chelle didn't seem flustered. "Trust me. We just gotta find the right car. And we're right next to the perfect neighborhood to find it."

Next thing we knew, we were looking inside the garages of abandoned houses in Granite Bay. We didn't spend much time in each one; we rarely even entered a house. We just looked at the cars, quickly rummaged through the garage for any useful tools, and moved on to the next one.

After about two hours, we happened upon a nice two-story in a secluded cul-de-sac with a three-car garage. A BMW SUV and a Mercedes E350 sat untouched, but that's not what captured Chelle's interest. Chelle walked over to the third car, which was draped in a soft beige cover.

"Help me with this," she said to Cody, grabbing the front of the cover. The two of them flipped it up, which sent dust flying and exposed a bright red '57 Corvette. It was one of the most beautiful cars I'd ever seen.

Chelle opened the gas cap and smelled. "Let's just hope this is full."

"But won't the gas be bad by now?" Cody asked.

"Could be. But most people who collect cars like this like to leave the tank full so moisture doesn't build up in the tank. Plus, this baby has a carburetor, not fuel injection. These classic 'Vettes will burn anything!"

Cody and I looked at each other, confused by how she knew all of this.

Chelle saw our expressions and sighed. "Boyfriend. Foster care. Don't ask."

And with that, she sat down in the driver's seat and looked for the car keys.

Nothing.

We spent the next 15 minutes scouring the house for keys. Slippery went ahead of us, checking out each room. No strays. We looked in all of the normal places and came up empty.

After we'd combed the entire house, Chelle said, "Oh well, we'll have to do it another way." She then proceeded to crawl under the dashboard and began pulling out wires.

"You know how to hot-wire a car?" I asked.

She looked up at me and rolled her eyes. "I lived in foster care for 18 months. There are a lot of things I learned to do that I'm not proud of."

Cody and I laughed.

"Wow! *Grand Theft Auto* much?" Cody laughed again. "I never would have guessed."

Chelle stopped what she was doing for a second and looked up at us again. "Hey, I'm not that girl anymore. That was the old Chelle." Then she smiled as she got back to work. "But that doesn't mean those skills won't come in handy today."

With that, she touched two wires together and the starter cranked. The engine didn't even hesitate—it fired up immediately.

Cody opened the garage door and quickly scanned the street.

"All clear."

We all hopped in and I told Chelle, "You got it started—you drive!"

She smiled and gladly slid behind the wheel. Cody and I crammed in next to her. "Sorry, boy." We told Slippery. "No room for you." Slippery didn't look too upset. He ran into the backyard and laid down in the shade of a large oak tree, glad to be away from the 'Vette's roar.

With a press of the accelerator, the engine roared again, back-fired once or twice, but managed fine overall with that aged fuel. Chelle slammed the shifter into reverse, and within minutes we were buzzing up Highway 80 in a blast from the past.

It was a one-day trip. As the day progressed, we watched the gas gauge slowly move from full, to half, to a quarter tank. We ended up bringing it back to the house at day's end and parking it where we'd found it. We hoped we could find clean gas and take her for another run someday. But inside, we knew this had probably been a once-in-a-lifetime experience.

Chelle and I pulled the cover back over the car—it seemed like the right thing to do.

As we walked away, I put my arm around her shoulders and said, "I never would have imagined you could hot-wire a car. Wow."

Chelle smiled. "That was the old Chelle!" She pointed at herself. "You're looking at the new Chelle now."

As we walked down the road, I kissed her on the cheek. "I like the new Chelle."

JOURNAL ENTRY #17

///

Something to Think About
Back to Reality . . .

• Google Image a '57 Corvette and take a peek at what a beautiful car it is. If you could drive a classic car for a day, what car would you choose?

• When Chris and Cody discovered Chelle's past experience with stealing cars, Chelle made a point to tell the brothers, "That was the old Chelle." Why do you think she wanted to make that clear?

THE BIBLE PROVIDES SOME GOOD WISDOM:

"This means that anyone who belongs to Christ has become a new person. The old life is gone; a new life has begun!"
(2 Corinthians 5:17, NLT)

• According to the verse, what do those of us who've put our faith in Christ become?

• What's some of "the old" stuff in your life?

• When we put our faith in Jesus and stop living for the old stuff, what is it replaced with? What does this look like?

SOMETHING I CAN DO THIS WEEK:

If you've put your faith in Jesus, write out your story on a piece of paper. Write down what your life was like before you met Jesus, what you did specifically to put your trust in him, and what your life is like now.

If you haven't taken this step of faith yet, you can do it right now. And then Jesus will give you a new beginning. Just pray in your own words and tell him, "Jesus, I don't want to do the old things that I used to do. I want to put my trust in you. Forgive me for my sins. Make me new." Start this new life by getting to know Jesus better. Read his Word. Start with the book of Matthew.

CRYING IS BETTER THAN DYING

We met Stan lost October . . . and he was a mess.

Poor Stan had just lost his wife and kids.

Most survivors lost loved ones right away. Cody and I did. But Stan and his wife Nancy managed to survive with their twins, Brianna and Britney, for the first few years.

Stan was a rancher near Gridley, a small rural town north of Sacramento. And he was used to fighting off predators after 30 years of raising cattle and sheep.

Stan's girls were strong too. Growing up on a farm, they'd been doing heavy lifting and chores since they were able to walk. Stan told us Britney killed her first buck at age 10, and she'd been chukar hunting since she was eight and got her first 20-gauge.

Brianna had been hunting a few times, but she preferred to help Nancy around the house. This didn't exclude her from doing chores, however. At 13, the twins could throw 75-pound hay bales into the back of the pickup, drive it out to the meadow, and feed the cattle. They knew it helped put food on the table.

When The Havoc started, Stan quickly secured the house and the barn, boarding up the windows on the lower level and fortifying the doors. He moved six head of cattle and a handful of sheep into the barn with the horses, not knowing this chaos would last for years. Within the first few months, the strays got every piece of livestock that wasn't inside the barn. Stan was able to stretch the supply of barn meat for about a year. (It would have lasted way longer than that if they'd had refrigeration.) After that, he was left with two horses, a goat for milk, and a handful of chickens.

One day Stan was out hunting, trying to bring home some duck for dinner. The girls were feeding the chickens in the farmyard and didn't notice a group of strays that had wandered out from the timber and were headed for the barn.

Stan had strung barbed wire around the property, which kept most of the strays tangled up for a day or so. (And then he'd go out later and dispose of them properly.) But that morning a 300-pound stray became tangled in the fence, fell, and brought down most of the barbed wire down with him. The others just stepped over the stray and marched onto Stan's property without difficulty. The girls were caught off-guard and were quickly overrun. Nancy heard their screams, ran outside, and saw the whole thing.

Stan had experienced a lot of death while growing up on the farm; he'd even lost his parents a few years back. But the loss of his daughters gripped him and Nancy like something they'd never experienced before. Everything they'd done on the farm was for Brianna and Britney. Those two girls were their life. And life just didn't seem worth living without them.

That's probably why Nancy did what she did. One morning when he returned to the house after clearing the perimeter of strays, Stan found his wife hanging from the rafters in the barn.

Stan didn't cry. He just began digging a third grave.

We happened upon Stan a few weeks after this happened. He was a tough man, but we could see something was eating him from the inside out. He gave the three of us shelter for a few nights and eventually shared his story. As much as he tried to convince us he was "used to death" and this "didn't bother him," we knew better.

On the third day, Slippery and I went with him on his morning walk to check the fence around his property. As we talked, the subject of my parents came up.

"I'm assuming . . . they're . . . gone?" he asked carefully, as we stepped over a small creek.

I thought for a moment, considering exactly how much I wanted to share with the man. It was the most painful memory of my life—something I didn't exactly enjoy recalling and reliving. But Stan obviously understood pain. He was a new resident to the hell I'd been occupying for almost four years now.

"Yeah. It happened about a week after The Havoc started," I began, not sure how much of this story I'd unravel. "When we first saw what was going on, we gathered in the living room and made a game plan. The news stations were unveiling the insanity of the situation, so we started gathering supplies and inventorying our food."

"I remember that week well," Stan remarked.

"We didn't know how safe it was. Every once in a while we'd peek out the windows and see strays walking around outside," I explained.

"Strays, eh?" Stan commented. "I haven't heard that name. We called them 'Uglies.'"

I laughed and said, "That's pretty fitting. Well, when the streets looked clear, my dad and I made a couple of food runs that first week. The stores were insane. People didn't even bother paying anymore; they just grabbed stuff off the shelves. My dad didn't feel right about that, so he talked with Bruce, one of the grocery checkers, and asked him what to do. Bruce told us to grab whatever we needed.

"The checkers didn't try to stop anyone after the first few days. Only Bruce and one of the store managers bothered to show up at the store after the first week, just to check on things. They saw what was going on and wisely decided to assist people and create some order. They handed carts to people and literally told them to 'fill 'em up.' Most people didn't argue.

After a week, the stores near us were empty. So bands of looters began going from house to house. That's something else we learned right away," I said, pausing and looking at Stan. "The strays weren't the only enemies we needed to fear."

I resumed walking, watching Slippery navigate the long grass in a zigzag formation in front of us, occasionally stopping whenever he caught the scent of something interesting.

"When we saw the looters arrive on our street, my parents quickly sent Cody and me up to the attic with a box of provisions and our 12-gauge. We heard the door get kicked in about an hour later."

I paused as I remembered that moment when I was sitting in the attic, listening.

Then I described for Stan what I'd heard, "There were raised voices . . . and then three shots. Cody was barely 12 at the time, and he started crying. I held his face to my chest and motioned for him to be silent. We heard sounds of rummaging throughout the house for the next hour or so . . . and then deafening silence.

"We waited in the attic for hours. Cody eventually fell asleep as he leaned against me. I remember just staring at the attic door, longing to see my dad's head pop up and hear his familiar voice assure me that everything was okay. He never came up."

I took a breath. "When we emerged from the attic, the house

was in shambles. Every mattress was flipped over, every drawer dumped out. The pantry was empty, and even a bunch of my dad's clothes were missing."

As I shared all of this with Stan, I reflected on the moment. My mom's jewelry had been untouched. I remember grabbing my mom's locket and my grandma's ring and shoving them in the pocket of my shorts. I didn't tell Stan those details.

The next part wasn't easy to talk about. And I hadn't shared it with many people. But as Stan and I walked, the words flowed pretty easily. For some reason it's easier for me to talk when I'm walking and looking forward.

Stan noticed my hesitation. "You don't need to talk about this if you don't want to."

"It's okay," I reassured him. "It's good for me."

I continued, "When Cody and I walked into the living room, we quickly discovered what those three shots had been—exactly what I'd feared but hadn't allowed myself to believe. My parents' bodies were lying together—my dad's just in front of my mom's. I didn't think about it then, but I've reflected on that image countless times since . . . the way they were lying there . . . the way they fell. I think he stood in front of her, trying to protect her. He was shot first—once in the chest, and then in the head. And then they shot her once in the head, and she fell on top of him.

Cody ran over to their bodies, sobbing and hugging them. I let him have his moment, but I held back my emotions. I knew I had to be the strong one now." I looked over at Stan when I said this.

"For the next week, Cody cried himself to sleep every night. I feigned like it hadn't affected me, but I was dying inside.

"It was just me and Cody, so I didn't have anyone to turn to for comfort. Usually my mom was there for that." I paused a moment to take it all in. "But now she was gone."

"Three days later, I picked up my Bible to search for some comfort. That's where my dad had always gone. My dad's worn Bible fell open to a verse in 1 Peter chapter 5 that said, 'Cast all your anxiety on him because he cares for you.'

My first thought was, 'Sure . . . if only it were that easy.'

Then I remembered something my dad had told me. 'Chris, don't just read one verse. Read the context. See what the verses around it have to say. Then you'll discover what the author's intent was.'

So I backed up just a little bit and read the whole passage. It said, 'All of you, clothe yourselves with humility toward one another, because, "God opposes the proud but shows favor to the humble." Humble yourselves, therefore, under God's mighty hand, that he may lift you up in due time. Cast all your anxiety on him because he cares for you.'

I've heard people quote that 'cast your anxiety' verse a bunch, and I always wondered if they've ever read how to do it. Because to me, the 'how' is pretty important. After my parents died, I was hurting and didn't want anxiety. The key for me was 'how' to get rid of it.

I've thought about this a lot," I said, and then I stopped walking and looked at Stan. He seemed to be taking in what I was saying. I continued, "I think what God is saying there is that we have to get rid of our pride—any part of us that thinks we can do it ourselves. That's tough for me to do. But if we really want God to comfort us, we need to tell him, 'Okay, God. I *can't* do this on my own. I'm giving this to you.'

"So that's what I did—I gave it all to him. I did what those verses said. I humbled myself and said, 'Please take this anxiety from me. It's obvious that it's too much for me to handle.' When I prayed that, my tough exterior layer was peeled back, and I began to cry. I cried harder than I'd ever cried before."

When I'd finished telling Stan my story, I wiped tears from my cheeks. The two of us walked along in comfortable silence. There was nothing left to be said.

Two days later, the three of us packed up our gear and thanked Stan for his hospitality. He offered to let us stay, but we kindly declined. "You've got a beautiful home here, Stan, and we can't thank you enough for your hospitality," I told him. "But we're thinking there may be a community of people out there somewhere who've carved out a life for themselves, working together to protect and provide for each other. We're keeping our eyes on the horizon."

"I've wondered that myself."

"Why don't you come with us?" I offered.

Stan looked over toward the three graves on his property. "Thank you. Really. I appreciate the offer. But this is home for me."

He gave us a few weapons, including a Smith & Wesson 7-shooter, a revolver that held seven bullets instead of six. We thanked him again and he shook it off, "It's nothing. I'm glad to help."

As we stepped off the porch, Stan put his hand on my shoulder. "Chris."

I paused.

He looked at me with tears in his eyes. "Thanks."

His eyes said paragraphs more. I knew his struggle. I'd been there myself. I was still there at times. But God carried me through, and I knew he would carry Stan as well.

With the sun over our right shoulders, we walked down the road. My pack was a little heavier, but my burden seemed lighter.

JOURNAL ENTRY #18

//

Something to Think About
Back to Reality . . .

- How do you deal with sad situations?

- Why did Stan and Chris think it was better to hold their feelings inside?

- What did they need to do to deal with their grief?

THE BIBLE PROVIDES SOME GOOD WISDOM:

"All of you, clothe yourselves with humility toward one another, because, "God opposes the proud but shows favor to the humble." Humble yourselves, therefore, under God's mighty hand, that he may lift you up in due time. Cast all your anxiety on him because he cares for you." (1 Peter 5:5-7, NIV)

- With what does Peter tell us to clothe ourselves? What might this look like?

- What did Chris find in the verses that helped him learn "how" to get rid of the anxiety that was overwhelming him in grief?

- How does humbling ourselves before God free us to receive his help?

- Did Chris's story help you like it helped Stan?

SOMETHING I CAN DO THIS WEEK:

Pray and ask God specifically for humility this week. Ask him to show you what it looks like to live life with "him in charge." Then pray for specific situations that you'll encounter and ask God for wisdom on how to approach those situations in humility, demonstrating God's power in your life, not your own.

ENJOY THAT DRINK...
IT WILL BE YOUR LAST

Last week we met a really kind man named Ben. When we discovered him, he was stranded on top of the ranger's kiosk at Discovery Park, where the American River flows into the Sacramento River just outside of downtown Sacramento. About a dozen strays were gathered around the booth, reaching up toward Ben in an effort of futility. The man was out of reach, but he was also trapped. There was no getting down from there without help.

Cody and Slippery went to work.

They quietly walked up and stopped about 30 yards from the kiosk. Cody began jumping up and down and waving his hands. It was surprising how long it took the preoccupied group to notice Cody and Slippery. But eventually, a few of the raggedy bunch noticed them and began running toward Cody.

Cody, who had his bow and arrow ready, shot one stray at 20 yards. It dropped and then four strays immediately began ravaging their fallen comrade. Cody shot two more of them before the group got within 10 yards of him.

Then Cody released Slippery. "Go to it, boy!"

Slippery ran left and Cody ran right. Three strays chased the pup, and four others pursued Cody.

Chelle and I didn't waste a second. We ran up to the kiosk to greet the tired stranger, offering him a hand down. He gladly accepted our help.

"How long were you up there?" I asked, as we jogged toward

the path along the river. I knew the path offered protection. We could always jump in the river if needed.

The stranger breathed heavily, apparently weak from hunger and thirst. "Three days . . . I think." He stopped to catch his breath. "My water ran out yesterday. Got any?"

Chelle handed him her canteen. "I'm Chelle."

The stranger nodded, gladly accepting the canteen and guzzling from it. After he drank half the water, he wiped his mouth. He was breathing heavily. "Chelle? Is that like . . . short for Michelle?"

"For some," Chelle replied. "But the name 'Chelle' is on my birth certificate."

"Nice," he said, taking another sip. "I'm Ben. It says 'Benjamin' on my birth certificate." He managed a smile between raspy breaths.

We walked along the river path with Ben for the next half hour before stopping to rest at the stump where we'd arranged to meet Cody. Ben was from Stockton, but he'd made his way north, staying close to the river. We weren't the only ones who'd discovered the strays' ineptitude at navigating moving waters.

"We got pretty good at fishing," he said. "One of the few food sources that hasn't disappeared yet."

"We?" I asked.

"Yeah. My buddies Perry, Kevin, Van, and me." He sighed. "They didn't make it. They liked drinking a little too much."

Chelle and I didn't say anything. It never seemed appropriate to interject an opinion when someone is talking about the people they've lost.

"Not too smart to get drunk these days," Ben continued. "If you're gonna drink 'til you pass out, you might as well just lie down on a plate." He laughed. "Plus, you're already marinated and ready to go!"

We'd seen plenty of people turn to alcohol during the first few months, and their lives were quickly cut short. In the old world, drinking was practically celebrated. If something good happened, "Raise your glass!" If people drank too much, "Sleep it off." The only time drinking alcohol seemed to be frowned upon was if you got behind the wheel after.

These days, the laws of nature were simple: If you put something in your body that impairs your judgment, you die.

Cody and Slippery showed up a few moments later. "Lost 'em," Cody said, as he doubled over with his hands on his knees, and tried to catch his breath. Then he looked up and smiled. "The two that are left, anyway." He reached over and scratched Slippery on the top of the head. "Isn't that right, boy?"

Slippery raised his head to enjoy the scratch and then resumed his panting.

"Someone give that dog a drink!" Ben said. "Water, that is." He smiled.

Ben thanked Cody and Slippery effusively. We camped with him for a few nights and swapped stories. He taught us about fishing, and we taught him a few things about evading strays.

After we said our good-byes, I asked Chelle, "What'd you think of Ben?"

"He was nice. A good fisherman," she commented. "I don't think I would have liked his friends too much."

"Oh?" I asked.

"Yeah," Chelle said. "My uncle drank a lot." She paused and looked away for a few seconds.

"'Nuff said."

JOURNAL ENTRY #19

///

Something to Think About
Back to Reality . . .

• Why did Ben's friends die?

• In Chris's world, impairing your judgment by drinking too much alcohol could mean death. What does drinking too much lead to in our world?

THE BIBLE PROVIDES SOME GOOD WISDOM:

"For you are all children of the light and of the day; we don't belong to darkness and night. So be on your guard, not asleep like the others. Stay alert and be clearheaded. Night is the time when people sleep and drinkers get drunk. But let us who live in the light be clearheaded, protected by the armor of faith and love, and wearing as our helmet the confidence of our salvation." (1 Thessalonians 5:5-8, NLT)

• Why do you think this passage tells us to "stay alert and be clearheaded"?

• This isn't the only place where the Bible warns us to avoid drunkenness. In Ephesians 5:18, Paul says, "Don't be drunk with wine, because that will ruin your life. Instead, be filled with the Holy Spirit" (NLT). Why does the Bible consistently warn people against drunkenness?

• What are we to be filled with instead? How can we do that?

• How do these passages apply to your life?

SOMETHING I CAN DO THIS WEEK:

Write down three specific ways you can allow God to "fill you" this week.

LITTLE CABIN IN THE SNOW

Life as a nomad gets old fast. It's hard living without a place to call home.

Before The Havoc, I never imagined that one day I'd carry everything I own in a backpack. But that's reality. We've never stayed in one location for more than a few months. The food supply and the need for safety pushes us from place to place.

That's why I'm continually looking for that one special place, a place where people like us can live together in safety . . . a place we can call home.

This quest drove us north toward Lake Tahoe in the Sierra Nevada Mountains. Our intended destination was a cabin in Kings Beach, a small village on the north shore of the lake. I'd visited the cabin with my family before The Havoc. The cabin belonged to our friend Bob, and I knew where he hid the key under the porcelain frog in the side yard.

I got the idea last winter when we got stuck in an early snowstorm in Colfax (not even an hour outside of Sacramento), heading up the Sierra Nevadas. Colfax usually doesn't get hit hard with snow, but this particular October night brought about six inches. We found shelter in a small house set on a hill, and that week we discovered two things:

1. Refrigeration
Cody shot a deer, which was more than enough meat to feed us for a week . . . if only we had a refrigerator. Typically, we'd eat as much as we could during the first 24 hours, make as much jerky as possible, and inevitably some meat would spoil. Life

was difficult in a world without power.

But the freezing temperatures gave us some new options. We turned an upstairs bedroom into a walk-in freezer of sorts. We opened both windows, which allowed that room to get down to about 30-something degrees. We kept our deer carcass in there, refrigerated, and it was out of the reach of critters. We ate venison steaks for a week!

2. Strays Are Helpless in the Snow

On one of our hunting outings, we encountered a pack of strays eating the remains of a rabbit. Normally, I would've used my machete on them because Chelle and I can't always outrun the faster ones. But these strays couldn't navigate the snow very well. It was actually quite comical. They looked like toddlers attempting their first steps.

We told Cody about this, and he decided to do a little recon. Sure enough, strays can't keep their balance in the snow, and they're easy to dispose of once they're disoriented.

That little mountain experience stirred our thinking. If we could find a nice cabin, we could really use snow to our advantage. That's when I remembered my friend Bob's place.

So we began our trek to Lake Tahoe to see if Bob's cabin was safe.

Luckily, the October weather returned to its typical temperatures. Not warm by any means, but not snowy and freezing either. It took about a week to make the journey. It probably wasn't much more than 50 miles, but it was an uphill climb the entire way, and we had to go over the Donner Pass, which is a story in itself.

The journey certainly wasn't easy. It takes time to move cautiously every day, leaving time to hunt and cook at night. It was almost November when we finally arrived. And as the elevation grew, the temperatures dropped. If Bob's cabin wasn't available, we'd need to find someplace else to stay—and fast.

When we first arrived on the little mountain road, everything looked abandoned. No sign of humans or strays. Bob's cabin sat at the top of a hill with a beautiful view of Lake Tahoe and the small town below. We released Slippery and he went exploring. Within 10 minutes, he was back. Usually that meant he hadn't discovered anything. We decided to wait until dark before taking a closer look. We've found it's often better to do recon under the blanket of darkness.

We snuck around the backside of the cabins, circling the entire neighborhood. We didn't see any lights or movement of any kind. We eventually found our way back to Bob's cabin and settled into some juniper bushes with a clear view of several cabins.

After sitting for an hour, Chelle's teeth began chattering. She pulled Slippery closer to her, holding him tight and trying to get warmth from his body. Chelle is always cold; it's probably because she has no body fat.

"How cold do you think it is?" Cody finally asked.

"Too cold!" Chelle said. "The cabin looks safe. Let's do this."

I couldn't argue. We hadn't seen a single sign of danger. So I crept over to the side of the house and the place where I'd last seen the porcelain frog years ago. I knew finding the key would be much better than breaking a door or window.

It took only about three minutes of digging in the moonlight before I located the frog. I lifted him up and . . . eureka! The key was still there.

Three minutes later, Cody unlocked the back door and stuck his head inside. He took a big whiff and immediately wrinkled his nose and turned back to look at us. "Phew!" Cody whispered. "Strays!"

Cody closed the door again quietly, and we reconvened behind the juniper bushes.

"What do you think?" Cody asked. "It definitely smells like strays."

I looked to Cody and Chelle for their opinions, but I could barely make out their expressions in the moonlight. They just looked back at me as if I was supposed to decide.

"Well," I finally offered. "This place is probably worth the risk."

Chelle and Cody listened as I explained my reasoning. "The place looks isolated. That's worked well for us in the past. The town isn't very populated, which is always a safe bet. And the cold is going to help us preserve any game we kill."

I continued, "The cabin is on top of a hill with a great view of everything coming from almost a mile off." I gestured to the street below. "It's a great vantage point."

I shrugged. "Honestly, if there are a few strays in there, it's nothing worse than what we've dealt with countless times. The three of us can handle it."

Cody stroked Slippery's head. "The four of us!"

I chuckled. "I agree." I gave Slippery a scratch behind the ears, just where he liked it.

I turned to Chelle and Cody. "We live in a dangerous world,

and we've been dealt some pretty difficult situations. But I've gotta say . . . there's no one I'd rather walk through that door with than you two."

I held out my hand, palm down, and asked them to join me. Cody put his hand on top of mine, and Chelle put hers on top of Cody's. Smiling, Cody reached over and put Slippery's paw on top of our stack of hands.

"Let's do this," Cody said.

He led us to the door and opened it carefully. Slippery slipped inside to check it out.

From our vantage point on the back porch, we could see Slippery combing the main room, sniffing every corner. Nothing. After a quick survey of the kitchen, he disappeared upstairs. We took that as our cue to move into the cleared area.

As we stepped inside the cabin, our nasal passages were flooded with the stench of fecal matter and . . . something else. It's hard to differentiate stink, but this smelled different.

We paused just inside the back door, allowing our eyes to adjust to the dark cabin. Cody had his bow drawn, and Chelle and I each had our machetes ready.

All of a sudden, Slippery began barking madly from upstairs. It was the bark he commonly gave when he'd found something, not when he was warning an aggressor.

We cautiously moved up the stairs. I was in the lead, Cody was in the middle with an arrow pulled back and ready to fire, and Chelle watched our six.

Chelle wasn't in the back because she's a girl; Chelle was in the back because we trust her and she's lethal with a machete.

I'd seen her take out three strays in a matter of seconds—all by herself. And they weren't those sluggish ones either, but the frenzied sprinters with gnashing teeth. But that's not too surprising. After all, before we met her, Chelle had survived completely on her own for two years in this unforgiving world.

When we reached the top of the stairs, we could see Slippery, bathed in moonlight, standing inside one of the bedrooms and barking at a built-in cupboard under a bay window.

We slowly crept up next to Slippery.

"Good boy," I said, reaching out with my left hand to stroke Slippery's head. My machete was drawn, and I didn't take my eyes off the cupboard under the window seat.

The stench was stronger now, and as I looked down at the floor, I could see why. I was standing in fecal pellets. They weren't big enough to be human. And there was another smell—wet fur!

Suddenly, one of the cupboard doors burst open and something dark and furry darted toward our legs. The beast bypassed Slippery, Cody, and me before heading straight for Chelle, who was now standing in the doorway. Without hesitation, Chelle swung her machete downward, sinking the blade into the animal's back. With a squeal, the masked creature fell at her feet.

Chelle had killed a raccoon.

"Nice," Cody joked. "You killed Meeko."

Cody and I laughed, but Chelle never cracked a smile. "I hated that movie," she said as she pulled her machete out of the rodent's hide.

Two hours later, we were dozing in the living room downstairs.

The next day we discovered that something had chewed a hole through the side of the house in one of the upstairs bedrooms. And "Meeko" apparently made himself at home throughout most of the upstairs. We patched up the hole with some plywood we found in the garage, cleaned the wood floor upstairs (which was a huge job), and secured the cabin against any other predators that might visit.

We eventually converted one of the upstairs rooms into our refrigerator, complete with meat hooks and a drain. It was nice to have a place where meat would last for a week—rabbit, possum, turkey, deer, and even raccoon. We weren't picky. We were just thankful for food.

This cabin became our primary winter spot. We rarely encountered strays there; and better yet, we rarely encountered humans.

Humans were far more dangerous.

JOURNAL ENTRY #20

///

Something to Think About
Back to Reality . . .

• Make a menu of what you'd eat for the next three days if you could eat only items that were not refrigerated.

• Describe a time when you were really scared. Who was with you?

• Chris told Cody and Chelle, "We live in a dangerous world, and we've been dealt some pretty difficult situations. But I've gotta say . . . there's no one I'd rather walk through that door with than you two." Who are the people with whom you feel safe?

• Why is it nice to have someone with you when you're scared or when you're facing danger?

THE BIBLE PROVIDES SOME GOOD WISDOM:

"Let us think of ways to motivate one another to acts of love and good works. And let us not neglect our meeting together, as some people do, but encourage one another, especially now that the day of his return is drawing near." (Hebrews 10:24-25, NLT)

• What do you think the author of the verse is trying to encourage us to do?

• Why do some people stop going to church or hanging out with Christians who will encourage them in their faith?

• Who are some people who are an encouragement to your faith in God and who motivate you to do right?

SOMETHING I CAN DO THIS WEEK:

Call or text a Christian friend right now and make plans to connect this week. When you get together, share what you learned about this verse and how you realized that he or she has been an encouragement to your faith. Talk about how you can both stay connected to God's people through church, Bible study, and good friendships.

SAYING THANKS

"Wow. It doesn't get much better than this," Chelle said, as she sat down at the small kitchen table in our cabin.

It was Thursday, November 28, according to Cody's calendar. That meant it was Thanksgiving Day. But we didn't need a special day to remind us to say thanks. We were thankful *anytime* we had something to eat.

When I was in fifth grade, I learned the importance of saying thank you. And I learned it the hard way.

My fifth grade teacher decided we should all practice giving an oral presentation, and she told us to share something with the class that was really special to us. I decided to share about my memory box.

I was a sentimental child. Call me awkward, if you will, but I treasured items like notes from my mother, my first fishing lure from my dad, and my grandpa's pocketknife. My dad noticed this, so he built me a wooden box to hold these mementos.

The box wasn't fancy. It was made of pine boards, dowelled and glued, and completely sealed. Then he used a jigsaw to cut the lid, adding two simple brass hinges. As a finishing touch, he engraved my initials on the lid with a router.

When I gave my presentation to the class, I couldn't help but notice that Alison Williams seemed really interested in my box.

Alison Williams was amazing! She had dark brown eyes, short brown hair, perfect lips, and smooth skin that always seemed to be tan—even during the winter (she was a swimmer). She'd never paid attention to me before . . . until that day.

After I gave my presentation, Alison approached me during recess and asked, "Where'd you get that box?"

I was a little surprised that she was talking to me. "Uh . . . my dad and I made it," I said. "He makes lots of things. We made the dresser in my room, and . . . "

She didn't let me finish my sentence, which was probably a good thing. I tend to ramble when I'm nervous. "Could you make me one?" she asked.

I was surprised once again, but I wasn't about to let this opportunity pass. "Sure. Easy."

It wasn't easy. But I wanted her to think I was good at something.

That night at dinner I told my dad I wanted to make a box for someone. I'd gone out to the garage and picked out some pieces of pine from the scrap pile. Dowels and glue were cheap, so I knew the only issue would be time.

"Sure," he said, wiping his mouth with a napkin. "It'll be fun."

The two of us cut the pieces that night, glued them together, and clamped them tight. "Let this dry till morning," he reminded me. "Tomorrow we can cut the lid, stain it, and finish it up."

I couldn't wait. And apparently neither could Alison.

Sure enough, the next day during lunch recess Alison asked me, "You're gonna build me a box, right?"

"Already started it," I told her proudly.

She seemed surprised, then smiled. "Cool."

That evening when my dad got home, we cut out the lid, engraved the initials "A. W." on the top of it, and added a light stain. After dinner, I added the first coat of varnish. I added a second coat right before bed.

I finished the box the next night, adding a final coat of varnish and beautiful brass hinges. The box was perfect. Better than mine, even.

I had trouble sleeping that night. What would Alison think of the box? I just knew that she was going to be so happy!

Finally, morning arrived. I carefully wrapped the box in newspaper and put it inside my backpack. I couldn't wait to see the look on Alison's face!

When I arrived at school, I went out to the blacktop to see if I could find her. It took me a few minutes, but I finally spotted her talking with her best friend Jen.

I walked over and pulled off my backpack. "I brought you your box."

"Really?" She seemed excited.

I pulled the box out of my backpack and unwrapped the newspaper. Her eyes grew bigger as I handed her the box and she ran her fingers over the engraved initials. She opened the lid and looked at all four sides, admiring it.

I didn't know what to do in the awkward silence, so I zipped up my backpack.

Then she said it, "I didn't think you'd actually make it, but Jen bet me you would." She shrugged. "Guess I was wrong." Then she walked away.

That was the last time she ever spoke to me.

I think about that moment often and how it made me feel. I didn't need money, a trophy, or a kiss (although I gladly would have accepted any one of those). But a simple "thanks" sure would have been nice.

Until that moment, I never realized how much someone's thanks meant.

And it wasn't until The Havoc started that I really started thanking God.

That might sound absurd—thanking God when everything went bad. But I guess that's because it wasn't until things were really bad that I realized how much I need him.

It's funny, but when I was a kid, my parents taught me to pray before every meal. Their intentions were good; but in all honesty, prayer felt like a chore. It was something we were "supposed to do" before eating. My mom would put a nice hot plate of tuna noodle casserole under our noses, and then my dad would say a long prayer—all while the aroma of the food seemed to torture us. I don't think I ever listened to the prayer. I just wanted the food!

Besides, I don't know how thankful I really was back then. Whenever I wanted food, I'd just open the fridge and there it was. What was there to be thankful for?

It's mind-blowing to even reminisce about those days. We had no idea how good we had it. We had no idea how thankful we should have been.

Now, the three of us always pray when we get a meal—not because we have to, but because we're truly thankful. Cody, Chelle, and I have gone three or four days without eating anything more than a few grasshoppers. Then Cody would catch sight of a squirrel. Two hours later, before sharing a few ounces of squirrel meat, we'd pray and truly thank God for his provision.

Prayer isn't just a ritual anymore.

Now it's Thanksgiving Day. We're sitting inside a warm cabin, we're safe, and we have water to drink and a few ounces of squirrel meat to eat. Added bonus: I have Cody and Chelle sitting right here next to me. I don't think I've ever been so thankful in my life.

JOURNAL ENTRY #21

//

Something to Think About
Back to Reality . . .

• What's something you made that you were really proud of?

• Describe a time when you gave a gift and the receiver seemed ungrateful for it.

• Describe a time when someone gave you a gift and you were ungrateful.

THE BIBLE PROVIDES SOME GOOD WISDOM:

"And when you pray, do not be like the hypocrites, for they love to pray standing in the synagogues and on the street corners to be seen by others. Truly I tell you, they have received their reward in full. But when you pray, go into your room, close the door and pray to your Father, who is unseen. Then your Father, who sees what is done in secret, will reward you."
(Matthew 6:5-6, NIV)

• How does Jesus describe how the hypocrites pray?

• How does Jesus tell us to pray? Why do you think this is important?

• Why do you think Jesus tells us that God sees what is "done in secret"? Is it easier to be honest with someone who's seen your innermost secrets?

• How have Chris, Cody, and Chelle's motives for prayer changed?

SOMETHING I CAN DO THIS WEEK:

Try something: go into your room and close the door. Don't tell anyone you're doing it. Then take a few minutes and just get real with God. Start by saying something like: "God, I know you already know everything about me, and that means that you saw me when I . . . " and see where that prayer takes you. Then truly thank God for all that he does for you.

RELATIONSHIPS FIRST

"Have you ever considered that your way might not be the best way, or are you too blind to see that?" Cody snapped.

It was our biggest argument in years.

We argued frequently. We're brothers. That's what brothers do. But it was typically small stuff:

"You're putting too much wood on the fire."

"No I'm not."

"Yes you are; it needs to breathe. Stop smothering it."

"Why don't you build it yourself then!"

But this argument was much more than that.

After years of surviving on our own, we were actually getting used to it. Hunting and gathering food was becoming a little easier, and thanks to places like our Tahoe cabin and a few houses along the river in Fair Oaks, we'd been enjoying a few comforts of indoor living.

Cody saw these comforts as the "end all" . . . the answer to what we'd been looking for. I thought they were just good stepping-stones until we found something better. I knew there had to be something better out there.

"There is no secret utopia, Chris! Let it go!"

Slippery slipped out of the room with his head down and crawled into the upstairs bathtub. Slippery always goes into the bathtub when voices rise.

"I'm not looking for utopia. I just don't want to limit our options. There have to be others out there just like us. And who's to say that some of them haven't joined together and created someplace good . . . someplace safe?"

Cody wasn't convinced. "That's a nice theory, but that's all it is—theory! So why should we leave something good right here for something highly improbable?" he shouted.

"You really think that in a world this big it's improbable for a group of good people to get together and carve out a life for themselves?"

"No. I think it's very probable." Cody gestured around the living room where he was sitting. "We've done it. It's right here. No need to look any further!"

"You're willing to sacrifice our future?"

Cody threw up his hands and walked around the room. "I was just about to ask you the same thing!"

"How am I giving up our future? I'm just sick of eating beetles and squirrels! If I have to share one more squirrel between us, I'm going to kill myself."

"I'll help you!" Cody quickly retorted.

Chelle, who'd been silent during all of this, stood up and screamed, "Enough!"

Her face was fiery red. Cody and I didn't say another word.

"You guys are pathetic. Seriously." Then she imitated us, "'I'm going to kill myself . . . I'll help'? Do you even know what it's like to want to kill yourself?" Chelle waited for an answer, but neither of us dared speak. "Do either of you know what it's like to have no one?" She paused again, exchanging glances with both of us. "No, you don't, do you? Because you guys have always had each other. Wake up, both of you! Because you don't know jack about what it's like to be completely alone, and you have no idea what it's like to just lay there every night and wish God would take your life so you wouldn't have to go through the horrible torture you'd just experienced for even one more minute."

She sat down on the couch and took a breath before continuing in a much quieter voice, "If you guys want to disagree, that's fine. But don't you dare utter words that you can't take back and talk like you wish you were alone. You have no idea what you're wishing for. You *have no idea* what you have *right here.*" She pointed to both of us while she said it.

She stared at the coffee table for a moment, and then her eyes wandered to a pair of dice from the Monopoly game we'd played the night before. She grabbed a die. "You guys can't decide what to do? Fine. I'll decide. And I'm not going to choose because I don't want either one of you thinking I'm siding with the other. You guys are both being jerks, so this die is gonna decide."

She paused. "So if I roll a one . . . " she stopped mid-thought, rethinking her logic.

"How about one to three we stay, and four to six we go," I suggested.

"Let's do odd or even," Cody interjected. "If we—"

"Shut it!" Chelle yelled. "You guys can't even agree on the roll of the die! I decide! One to three we stay, four to six we go. That's it. Agreed?"

She looked at us both, waiting for our support. We both nodded a little reluctantly.

"Now, don't either of you start whining if you don't get your way. Promise?"

Cody and I looked at each other. We both nodded again.

Chelle rolled the die on the monopoly board, knocking over three hotels in the process. The die landed on a five.

She looked at us. "I guess we pack up and leave tomorrow morning."

She started to leave the room, but stopped short, turning to face us again. "You know, I'm new to the Bible, so I don't know it very well yet. But if there's one thing I've learned—especially from all of those letters in the New Testament to the different churches full of new Christians—it's this: stop fighting. Don't let bitterness creep up between you. Love one another." She took a step toward us and spoke firmly, "In other words, I don't think God gives a care whether we stay or go, but I *know* he cares about how we treat each other."

She paused for a moment, letting her words sink in. "Out here, all we've got is each other. Don't you guys dare throw that away. Make amends."

With that, she turned and walked upstairs.

Cody and I didn't talk for a few hours. I think we both wanted to, but each of us figured that the first one to talk "loses."

Finally, I couldn't take it anymore. I walked into the upstairs room where he was sharpening his knife and sat down on the bed in front of him. He looked up at me for a second and then resumed sharpening his knife.

"She's right, you know," I offered.

"Yeah, I know." He slid his blade along the smooth stone with care, spitting on it to keep the stone wet.

I reached out and put my hand on his arm, stopping him for a moment. "I'm sorry. Truly. We do have each other, and we should never let any disagreement get in the way of that."

He looked up at me. "I know, I know. She's right."

He went back to sharpening his blade.

I got up and headed for the door. Cody spoke before I reached the threshold. "I'm sorry too, but Chelle was right about something else."

"What's that?"

"You are a jerk."

I smiled. "She said we're both jerks."

"Yeah . . . well, she was half right."

JOURNAL ENTRY #22

//

Something to Think About
Back to Reality . . .

• What's one of the worst arguments you've ever had with someone in your family?

• Who was more at fault?

• How did you handle it? Was it the best way to do it?

THE BIBLE PROVIDES SOME GOOD WISDOM:

"Therefore, if you are offering your gift at the altar and there remember that your brother or sister has something against you, leave your gift there in front of the altar. First go and be reconciled to them; then come and offer your gift." (Matthew 5:23-24, NIV)

• What does Jesus tell us to do if we're in a disagreement with someone? What does this mean? Why is this important?

• Why should we be reconciled with people before we worship Jesus and give him gifts?

• Who is someone with whom you need to reconcile?

SOMETHING I CAN DO THIS WEEK:

Contact the person whose name you wrote down for that last question and try to reconcile your relationship. This might take some humility on your part. Pray before embarking on this task, asking God to give you the strength and humility to do this.

TOUGH CHOICES

I've always loved the beach.

When I was a kid, my parents would take us to Santa Cruz Beach Boardwalk for one day each summer. Cody and I loved it! What more could you ask for: the ocean, the sand, and killer roller coasters.

Now the beach is almost just as appealing because it's practically stray-free.

Strays aren't afraid of anything, but they don't do well when trying to walk in the ocean or on the sand. Their balance is all whacky. So they usually stay inland as much as possible. This makes the ocean a great place to hang out—as long as you watch out for humans.

Cody, Chelle, and I headed down the California coast this past summer in search of possible living areas. On numerous occasions, people on the road had talked about an oasis in Southern Cal, a paradise with power, provisions, and people. In this bleak world, one can't help but dream about an oasis like that. It was probably just a rumor, but it was most definitely in the back of our heads as we made our way down the coast.

The California coast was fun. We started our journey in Los Gatos, avoiding San Francisco completely. Something we learned early on: never go near a major metropolis. Big cities are overrun with strays. It's best to stay at least 20 miles away from any significant city.

We camped a few nights in the redwoods, then made our way south, hitting Monterey, Morrow Bay, Santa Maria, and Santa Barbara. Santa Barbara was a little too populated near the beach, so we ventured a few miles south to Carpentaria and found a nice little avocado farm within sight of the ocean. It was so nice that we ended up staying there for a few weeks.

It was in June, which is surprisingly cold for a summer month. The California coastal residents would have called this "June gloom" back in the day. The fog hangs on for most of the day, sometimes not clearing out at all. This makes for 70- to 80-degree days on the California coast mid-summer. Whodathunkit? And for us, it was perfect! We lived in a world without air conditioning now and 70 to 80 degrees felt like paradise.

Soon we pressed on down The 101 to the beaches of Oxnard. People outside of California probably haven't heard of it. It's a small beach town next to Ventura, just north of Malibu and Los Angeles. We didn't plan on getting within 50 miles of L.A., knowing that would be suicide.

From Santa Barbara to Oxnard, the coast is lined with offshore oilrigs. Back before The Havoc, these were lit up at night and looked like little Christmas trees from the coastline. But now these huge structures were dark and rather ominous looking, especially when the moon hit them at night.

In July, we finally arrived at Oxnard and found something intriguing—an oilrig with its lights on.

It took a second for this to register because it used to be a common sight. But the power had been off for almost four years now. How was this thing juiced? Or more importantly, who was working this thing? One person can't man an oil rig.

We camped on the beach and talked about the ramifications of this discovery. "What if someone is making fuel? Could there be some form of government in place down here in Southern Cal that we didn't know about? What if this is the first sign of the power coming back on?"

That night I dreamt of movie theaters and pizza. Oh, how I missed both of those things.

Suddenly, I was awakened by the sound of a gun cocking. "Wakey, wakey!"

I opened my eyes to find a large Hispanic man standing over me with what looked like an AR-15 pointed at me. "How many of you are there? Are you part of a larger group?" He poked my chest with the gun.

It's one thing to see someone waving a gun around, but it's something else to have a high-powered assault rifle pointed at your chest. I was at a loss for words.

The man's eyebrows furrowed. "Habla Inglés?"

I finally mustered the power to speak. "Chill, man. I hablo. You had me at 'Wakey, wakey.' And we're alone. We're just looking for a place to stay."

The man wasn't alone either. He had two buddies, each with a gun pointed at us. Cody and Chelle woke up blinking, trying to adjust their eyes to the sunlight.

I looked over at Slippery. He was yawning and stretching. Nice watchdog! He'd proven to be pretty good at warning us about strays, but he rarely barked at humans.

The man with the gun took a step back and exhaled deeply, "Do you have any weapons?"

I thought about it. How much did I want to tell this guy? I soon answered my own question: as little as possible. I said, "Sure, just some bows and arrows, a couple machetes, and a few hunting tools."

The man adjusted his grip on his gun. "Let me see them."

Twenty minutes later, we were being escorted east along the beach with our hands on top of our heads. (The beaches ran east-west along this section of coast.) And within 10 minutes, we were walking past a huge factory snuggled right up next to the coast. I figured it was an oil refinery.

But then we heard and saw something unbelievable.

The factory was operating. Smoke was coming out of the red-and-white striped smokestacks.

Five minutes later, we passed some sand dunes and then came upon a pathway through the sand. The path led us to a huge metal gate surrounding a beautiful resort. It was a hotel re-sort from the Legacy Suites chain. I'd stayed at a few of these places as a kid. I always liked their breakfasts.

Good Belgian waffles.

Two other men met us at the gate. Both were wearing U.S. military uniforms. One of them spoke to our "friend" carrying the AR-15. "What have we got here, Enrique?"

"Three teenagers. Harmless. Two bows, two machetes, four knives, and a Smith & Wesson."

"And Scooby over there?" He nodded toward Slippery.

"Harmless."

"I'll tell Luke."

The guard left and was back in minutes with a large, tan man wearing shorts and a Semper Fi T-shirt. He opened the gate and extended his hand to me. "I'm Luke." There was no expression on his face at all.

I extended my hand, and he grasped it firmly, but politely.

"We don't see too many survivors these days," he said, sizing us up.

"True. And those we do meet seem to greet us with the same welcome spirit that you all have," I said a bit sarcastically.

"Oh," Luke said with a smirk, "you can't blame someone for taking precautions."

I ignored that. "How is that big oil refinery operating?"

Luke laughed. "That's not a refinery. That's a 560-megawatt power station. We've got 46 people manning that generating station, and 11 are out on the rig."

"Power station?" Cody asked. "We saw lights on out there. Do you have power here?"

Luke smiled. "Follow me."

I gave Slippery a quick pat on the head. "Stay here, boy. I'll be right back."

Luke and the two soldiers led us through the gate where we set our packs aside and meandered into the center of the re-sort. As we rounded the corner into the courtyard, we couldn't believe our eyes. About 12 people wearing swimsuits were lying around a beautiful pool filled with sparkling clear water. Beyond the pool was a grassy area with beautifully manicured trees. All of this was surrounded by rooms with balconies.

Luke turned to us, gesturing poolside, "Welcome to paradise."

Cody whispered to me, "Is now a good time to tell you that I was totally wrong about that whole 'there is no secret utopia' thing?"

A waiter brought drinks to two girls in bikinis lying on lounge chairs nearby. Luke grinned and teased one of the girls, "Not too many of those, Christy."

She laughed. "That's not what you said when we were doing shots last night." She took a sip and licked her lips. "Don't you like me when I'm tipsy?"

"I like you when you're anything," Luke replied. He turned back to us and said under his breath, "Get three drinks in that one and she'll do anything!"

Luke stepped into the corridor of a large building at the side of the pool. Cody shot me a skeptical look as we followed Luke over the threshold.

A large open room stretched before us. It was filled with tables and seemed to be a large eating area. In the middle of the room, men wearing white dinner jackets were setting up a huge buffet filled with strawberries, melons, and blackberries. I looked over at Cody. His mouth was wide open in shock.

Luke noticed us staring at the fruit buffet. "Prime, isn't it?" he said, raising an eyebrow. "We have several fields and orchards that we harvest. There's plenty for everyone. This is where we serve chow. Here." He grabbed three bowls and handed them to us. "Help yourselves."

Cody didn't hesitate to fill his bowl. Chelle and I were a little more skeptical, but it didn't keep us from filling our bowls too. I loaded up on berries.

"All of our people pitch in doing some kind of work," Luke

continued. "We have several squads of Marines, mostly from the base. They serve as guards."

We listened, but we were busy shoving fruit in our faces as we walked. I couldn't remember the last time I'd eaten fresh fruit like this. Sure, we'd find an occasional apple or orange tree. We'd even found berries along Lake Natoma. But there'd never been a veritable mix of fresh cut fruit like this.

"We've got people at the power station, people in the fields, cooks, a cleaning crew, dancers . . . "

"Dancers?" I asked.

"Yeah. Most of the girls here are dancers. The guys work hard; the girls keep them happy." He looked at Chelle. "You'd make a fine dancer. It's the easiest job here. Then you can lie around the pool all day like Christy and Jessica back there. Here, let me show you."

I exchanged a quick glance with Chelle. Her eyes told me all I needed to know.

Luke opened another door and music filled our ears.

Music! I hadn't heard music in probably three years. He led us into the room. The speakers were blaring an old-school dance mix.

*"She getting crunk in the club I mean she working
Then I like to see the female twerking . . ."*

The lyrics digressed from there. At first the sound was so refreshing, the beat was energizing. But as I looked into Chelle's eyes, I was embarrassed.

The room was laid out like a night club. It had a huge bar,

tables, and an enormous stage with a pole in the middle.

"Here's where it all happens," Luke said proudly, not even fazed by the lyrics. He leaned closer to Cody and me. "I told you this place was paradise. You guys will love it here. If you . . . "

I held up my hand. Luke stopped mid-sentence. "What?"

"This is amazing." I chose my words carefully. "I can't remember the last time I tasted fruit like this or heard . . . *music.*"

"I know, right?" Luke chuckled, giving me a friendly jab in the arm.

"But I need to talk with my brother and Chelle."

"Chelle." Luke repeated. He looked at her. "She's hot."

Watching his gaze, I quickly grabbed Chelle's hand and walked out the door with her. Cody followed.

We walked outside and headed for the gate. To the left, a group of guys were batting a volleyball around the pool. Two others had girls up on their shoulders, laughing and playing chicken. One of the girls pulled off the other girl's bikini top, and they both threw back their heads in laughter.

I pointed to the gate. "Cody? The gate?" Cody, now a little distracted, followed my lead and opened the gate.

Luke and his guys followed us. "So, how long do you guys need? Tonight's movie night, you know!"

Cody shot me a glance, looking for some sort of response. I kept walking.

We picked up our packs by the fence. When Slippery saw us, he stood and began wagging his tale. Enrique was standing outside the fence. I walked up to him. "Our weapons, please?"

Enrique looked at Luke.

Luke paused. He looked at me, then at Chelle, and back at me again. He exhaled loudly and gave Enrique a nod.

Enrique handed our weapons to us, and we wasted no time heading west along the beach.

I stole a quick glance back at the resort. The men stood watching us as we disappeared down the coast. They never moved from their post.

As we passed the dunes and the resort vanished from sight, Chelle stopped me. She looked into my eyes. "Thanks, Chris."

"For what?" I asked. I don't know why I asked it. I knew why.

Chelle looked down at her feet, fidgeting her right foot in the sand. Then she looked up at me. "For not selling out and for not asking me to sell out."

"I'd never ask you to do that . . . "

"I know," she said, putting a finger to my lips. Then she leaned in slowly and kissed me. It was the greatest sensation I'd ever felt in my entire life.

She resumed walking. Cody and I exchanged a quick glance and followed her.

About five minutes later, Cody asked, "What movie do you think they're showing?"

"Shut up, Cody."

JOURNAL ENTRY #23

//

Something to Think About
Back to Reality . . .

• Name some of the amazing elements of this paradise that Chris, Cody, and Chelle discovered.

• What were some of the warning signs that maybe this place wasn't right for the three of them?

• What did Chelle mean when she said, "for not selling out."

• In what ways do you think Chris, Cody, and Chelle might have had to "sell out" if they'd become a part of that community?

THE BIBLE PROVIDES SOME GOOD WISDOM:

"Remember, it is sin to know what you ought to do and then not do it." (James 4:16-17, NIV)

• What are some ways that people your age are tempted to do something they know they shouldn't do?

• What are ways that you, specifically, are tempted to do what you know you shouldn't do?

• How can you prepare yourself to do right in this situation?

SOMETHING I CAN DO THIS WEEK:

Write out a game plan to stand for what is right when you face tempting situations like the one you described above. Look up a passage of Scripture that details the truth about the situation, and then list some Christian friends who will help you stand for the truth.

EVERYTHING I NEED IS AT WAL-MART

Our journey back up the coast was bittersweet. We had tasted the fresh fruit, heard the music, and seen the cool water of the swimming pool. It was a glimpse of a world we'd once lived in, a world with power and convenience. But enjoying those pleasures in that community wasn't without a cost. So, we somberly headed north.

So much for finding a home.

We stuck to the coastline most of the way. The beaches provided a safe place to camp, plus the fishing was actually pretty good—especially off the abandoned docks.

After weeks of travel, we diverted inland before we reached San Francisco, stopping in a little suburbia called Fremont. It was there we discovered an abandoned Wal-Mart on the edge of town.

Many of the windows had been boarded up with plywood and reinforced with two-by-fours. All of the doors were locked. We used our bolt cutters to cut a chain on the front door.

With our machetes ready, we began surveying the empty store. Slippery ran ahead of us, sniffing as he went, and disappeared into the aisles. No barking—always a good sign.

The store had been completely looted of all food and supplies, with only a few miscellaneous toys and housewares remaining. Empty hangers hung from all the clothing racks, and the food shelves were completely barren. Even the Blu-ray movies and CDs were gone. Funny. A lot of good those things would do in a world without power.

One corner of the store showed signs of being lived in long ago. Someone had set up camp, complete with inflatable mattresses, sleeping bags, and small cooking supplies. A few empty cans of soup and plastic water bottles were thrown aside. Cody picked up one of the cans and smelled it. It had been picked clean by insects long ago, probably years ago.

Chelle ran her finger over the top of a dusty black TV stand, drawing a distinct line through the dust. Then she brushed her fingers off on her jeans.

The place looked like it hadn't been inhabited in a long time. A group of people had obviously secured the place early on and settled here, but it seemed like they'd left the building to go hunt—or do who-knows-what—locked the front door . . . and never made it back.

As Cody and Chelle began a second search of the store's shelves, this time in greater detail, I searched the makeshift living space. These people had left some useful supplies. The sleeping bags, although dusty, were newer and more resistant to colder temperatures. I intended to switch them with ours. They also had a couple of knives and a new frying pan.

As I rummaged through a small backpack resting by one of the sleeping bags, I heard a bizarre sound from the other side of the store—like something was rolling. Then I heard Cody and Chelle laughing. I got up and walked over to the main aisle, only to see Chelle, grinning from ear to ear, rolling toward me in a pair of rollerblades. She was holding another pair in her hands.

"Here. They're your size!" She tossed them at me, chuckling as she zoomed by. Then she reversed directions and skated backward through one of the aisles with ease.

"I didn't know you could rollerblade!" I shouted as she disappeared around the corner.

Her voice rang out from behind the empty shelves. "I used to do it every day. Anything to get out of that house!"

Sure enough, the skates were just my size. I laced them up and ventured after Chelle. On the first lap, I passed Cody who was now rummaging through a few tools scattered around in the auto parts section. He looked up as I rolled by. "You too?"

I'd worn rollerblades only a few times. They had a similar feel to ice skates, and I loved ice hockey. I can't say I was any good at it. You can't be good at ice hockey in Sacramento. It freezes only a few days a year, and there was only one good ice rink in town. So ice hockey was never on my list of potential scholarships.

I rounded another corner, making a loop in the perimeter aisles. Chelle passed me on the front aisle, easily turning and gliding backward again. She brushed her bangs out of her eyes and smiled at me, slowing down so I could catch up. I readily obliged.

She turned her head to navigate the next corner backward, then looked back at me, reaching out for my hands, pulling me close. My heart started racing.

Chelle and I had been through hell and back; we'd spent countless nights talking under the stars; really, we were best friends.

Part of me wanted something more.

She was striking in every way. I loved how her blonde hair constantly fell over her eyes. I loved the five freckles around her nose. (I'd counted them numerous times.) But her smile— that was the clincher. The left side of her mouth raised higher than the right side, like she was smirking, or perhaps she was scared to smile. But when she did, she lit up a room. It was a window into who she was. She lived in a broken world, but she wasn't beaten down. She had survived, and she hadn't let the tough times take away her joy.

Chelle looked up at me with her beautiful brown eyes. Time froze. We were gliding along as if floating on clouds, staring into each other's eyes. That's probably why we misjudged the next turn.

"Look out!"

My shout was too late. We both went tumbling into some boxes near the back of the store. Luckily, they were empty and provided a nice cushion for our fall. Actually, Chelle provided a cushion for my fall because I landed on top of her.

For a second the wind was knocked out of us, but then we burst out laughing. Our position was precarious. Chelle was laid out over several boxes with her head hanging lower than her body. I was blanketed over her with my chest in her face. I managed to prop up and crawl back to where my body weight wasn't crushing her anymore. Then we found ourselves in the exact same spot as before the crash—staring into each other's eyes, almost without interruption.

I closed my eyes and kissed her.

Our first real kiss had been that moment on the beach just a few weeks before. I couldn't forget that moment, but it was undefined. Was it just a thank you? Or was it something more?

This kiss was undoubtedly more. It was everything I'd felt for the last two years: *I love everything about you . . . I can't stop thinking about you . . . I can't imagine life without you.*

She grabbed my shoulders and kissed me as if we were still on that beach and had never stopped kissing. Fine by me. I didn't want to stop. But footsteps approached.

"What happened? I heard a crash and . . . " Cody ran up and then stopped mid-sentence. "Oh . . . wow."

We stopped when we heard Cody's voice, but we didn't scamper apart or try to play it off. We just turned our heads to look at him. Cody paused awkwardly.

"Um . . . I feel like I just walked in on my parents." And with that, he sauntered off.

Chelle and I looked at each other for a moment and then burst out laughing again. We crawled off the boxes, took off the rollerblades, and collected ourselves.

For two years we'd survived in this desolate, hopeless place. We'd spent two years living as friends, or as brother and sister . . . who really knows what definitions exist in this chaotic world? But now, hidden feelings had been exposed. Our relationship had grown into something more. The kiss said it all.

I killed the awkward silence. "We probably should figure out what we're going to eat today."

"Agreed," she replied.

We walked in the direction where Cody had disappeared, and I wondered, *Would things be different now, now that everything was in the open? Would she . . .*

Before I could even finish the thought, Chelle reached out and held my hand. I looked over at her, and the left side of her mouth raised ever so slightly.

Right then I knew that everything would be okay.

"I love you."

JOURNAL ENTRY #24

//

Something to Think About
Back to Reality . . .

• Who said "I love you"?

• Why did Chris and Chelle choose to rollerblade in the middle of a zombie apocalypse?

• Chris described Chelle as a person who lived in a broken world but wasn't beaten down. She "hadn't let tough times take away her joy." Have you ever met someone like that? Describe that person.

• How can we find joy during tough times?

THE BIBLE PROVIDES SOME GOOD WISDOM:

"Therefore, since we have been made right in God's sight by faith, we have peace with God because of what Jesus Christ our Lord has done for us. Because of our faith, Christ has brought us into this place of undeserved privilege where we now stand, and we confidently and joyfully look forward to sharing God's glory.

We can rejoice, too, when we run into problems and trials, for we know that they help us develop endurance. And endurance develops strength of character, and character strengthens our confident hope of salvation. And this hope will not lead to disappointment. For we know how dearly God loves us, because he has given us the Holy Spirit to fill our hearts with his love."
(Romans 5:1-5, NLT)

• What do problems and trials develop in us? What does endurance develop in us? What does character strengthen?

- Why does our hope of salvation (knowing that God loves us enough to save us) not lead to disappointment?

- Paul writes, "We know how dearly God loves us." How dearly *does* God love us? (Look up Romans 5:8.)

- How does God's love for us give us hope and, in turn, help us during our problems and trials?

- What might this look like in your life?

SOMETHING I CAN DO THIS WEEK:

This hope is available to us because of what Jesus did on the cross. How would you explain what Jesus did for you if someone asked you? How could you use Romans 5:8 this week to tell someone what Jesus did for you? And for that person?

First Peter 3:15 tells us to always be prepared to give an answer to anyone who asks us to give a reason for the hope that we have. Write out a simple paragraph explaining the hope you have in Jesus. Feel free to use verses like Romans 5:8 and John 3:16 to help you explain.

KNOW YOUR WEAKNESSES

Strays are relentless.

I don't know what it is. We haven't found an answer yet. No one knows why the dead won't quit being dead. All we know is that they're very dangerous, especially if they get to your neck.

After four years of surviving in this post-Havoc world, a person can grow careless. We're so used to strays lurking around every corner, it's almost tempting to become a little too casual with them. But that's when you're the most vulnerable.

The truth of the matter is, strays are a lot like mako sharks. They're unpredictable, they're rarely spooked, and once they set after something, they never stop.

So you never know what a stray's gonna do. Last week, we were walking along the American River bluffs and getting ready to do some fishing. A stray spotted us from on top of the bluffs, probably 70 feet above us. Without any hesitation, it leapt off the bluffs, spread eagle, and dove toward us. We stepped out of the way just before it hit the ground between us.

I'll never forget the sound; it's hard to describe. When's the last time you heard something that weighs 175 pounds hit the ground from 70 feet in the air?

The situation was only worsened by the angle at which it landed. The stray was coming down practically headfirst in some sort of slipshod, backwoods swan dive. So its spine snapped just below the neck, its body flipped over backwards, and its head remained hidden underneath its body. Then the body began twitching. It's probably the most disgusting thing I've ever witnessed . . . other than what happened next.

Two strays burst out of the trees not even 10 yards away from us. They were moving so fast, we didn't have time to pull out our machetes. They seemed to be heading toward Cody, who immediately put up his arms and protected his neck in a defensive maneuver. But they ran right past Cody and leapt onto the twitching corpse, furiously devouring it.

We crept away quietly while welcoming the nauseating distraction.

"I thought I was done for!" Cody finally said when we were about a mile down the path. "All I could do was protect my neck."

Strays always seem to lunge for the neck. There's no explanation for it, really, other than some weird animalistic instinct. But we've seen it happen enough times to know our weakness. If a stray gets your neck, it's game over.

Just a few days prior, we'd encountered a pack of strays behind the Save Mart shopping center near where Cody and I grew up. I don't know why we took the road behind the store. It was stupid, really. A wall stretches along one side, and the store sits on the other, creating a 200-yard alley. We'd walked about 100 yards when we heard footsteps behind us. We turned around to see five strays barreling toward us at full speed.

Everyone responded differently. Cody and Slippery took off running, which wasn't such a bad move because it lured three of them away from Chelle and me, leaving each of us to fight a single stray one-on-one. Unfortunately, the two that were still headed for us were huge. The one sprinting toward Chelle was easily twice her bodyweight. If it were to tackle her, she'd be done.

Mine was quicker than Chelle's. He leapt for me from about six feet away. I tried to move to the side, but his long arms caught me and brought me down with him.

It's hard to explain what goes through your mind at a moment like this. I know I was terrified, but I didn't have time to even fathom the situation. I just reflexively pushed the disgusting creature away as it lunged for my neck. Luckily, I got my left hand on its throat and locked my elbow, keeping its gnashing teeth away from me. Meanwhile, I reached for my knife with my right hand and plunged it into the corpse's temple a nano-second later.

By this time Chelle's stray leapt toward her. She didn't move aside at all; instead, she drew her machete and gave her best piñata swing. Her blade sank into its skull, but the momentum of its leap took them both down. She went down hard with a 200-pound lifeless stray on top of her. The stray was DOA as they hit the ground, but it slammed her against the pavement, scraping her up pretty good and knocking the wind out of her.

From where I still laid on the ground, I watched Cody sprint over to a dumpster. He leapt on top of the metal lid and drew his bow. Within seconds he took out the two strays that were chasing him, and then he took his time marking the one that was chasing Slippery. Cody whistled and Slippery headed toward the dumpster. As the stray chased Slippery head-on, Cody easily dropped it, hitting it right through the mouth.

I exhaled in relief. We'd made it once again. But who says we'd make it the next time? This time there were only five strays. What if there were six? What if two of them had attacked Chelle? The ending might have been totally different.

As we walked along the American River a week later, I looked over at Chelle. She still had some scratches on her cheek from where she hit the pavement behind Save Mart.

She moved her hair out of her face with her hand, caught me looking at her, and smiled.

What if something had happened to her?

Looking back at both of these situations, I realized we'd become a little cocky . . . or sloppy. Neither one was good. We were overconfident, and it almost cost us.

Our weakness wasn't our necks. Our weakness was our pride. We'd become too comfortable with dangerous situations, and now we were drifting into places that we never would have wandered through years before.

My weakness could have cost us our lives. I looked over at Chelle again. It could have cost her life.

I couldn't make that mistake again.

JOURNAL ENTRY #25

//

Something to Think About
Back to Reality . . .

• What's the most dangerous situation you've ever experienced?

• Looking back, is there something you could have done to avoid it?

• What did Chris finally identify as their true weakness? Explain how he came to that conclusion.

• What are ways people "get too comfortable" with temptations today?

• Pride tries to convince us we aren't vulnerable to temptations. We could talk about numerous temptations, but let's be honest: many people find it easy to give into the temptation of sexual sin. What are some specific ways this happens?

THE BIBLE PROVIDES SOME GOOD WISDOM:

"Run from sexual sin! No other sin so clearly affects the body as this one does. For sexual immorality is a sin against your own body." (1 Corinthians 6:18, NLT)

• What does this verse instruct us to do? How can we "run" from sexual sin? Give an example.

• What are some ways that you specifically might set yourself up for failure with sexual temptation?

• What is something you can do to "run" from this temptation before you even get into the situation?

SOMETHING I CAN DO THIS WEEK:

Sexual sin is one of those enticing sins, and it's difficult to steer away from it once we get in to deep. The key is not allowing ourselves to get into that situation in the first place. We should stay away from anything that causes us to fail in that area. That's why the Bible commands us to "run" away. Think of one step you can take this week, this month, this year to avoid putting yourself in a situation where you'll be tempted sexually. Do something today to take that step. (For example, if you decide to set a boundary where you don't browse the Internet in your room at night, then ask your parents to help you remove screens from your room.) If you don't struggle with sexual temptation, what's something that regularly tempts you and how can you run away from it?

THE HANSON INN

"It's not like we've got as much food as the people up there in the Hanson."

"What people up at the Hanson?"

It was the first time we'd heard about this place. For years now, I'd been keeping my eyes open for a safe community of good people. I'd practically discarded those hopes after our experience in Oxnard last summer, when we caught a glimpse of how some of these communities govern themselves. But this was new information.

"Up in Natomas, kinda near the airport," the man said, stroking his red beard. "Me and Jeff were there just last week. They fed us scrambled eggs. Haven't had scrambled eggs since... who knows when."

We met these two survivors under the Watt Avenue Bridge by the river. We'd spotted them fishing from a distance and had watched them for a while. They had three fishing poles between the two of them, so we approached and offered a trade. Slippery took the opportunity to play in the water while we bartered.

Cody offered them a nice buck knife and some jerky. They didn't seem to care about the knife, but the jerky made them think. After we sweetened the deal with a pair of gloves, they obliged, throwing in one of the salmon they'd just caught with the rod.

"How many were there?" I asked, wanting to find out more about this hotel. I had stayed at many of the Hanson Inns with my dad over the years. They were way better than the bargain motels, but not as expensive as you'd think. They'd always had very clean facilities with nice grounds.

"We never saw them all," Jeff answered. Then he turned to his red-bearded friend, Mickey. "How many did you see besides the big fella?"

Mickey didn't even skip a beat. "Probably 20. But that was all that showed up for breakfast."

"Were they nice?" I asked.

"A little sketchy," Jeff replied, picking salmon from between his teeth. "The big black guy calls himself Shiv. Apparently he was locked up in Folsom before all of this." Jeff smiled and said, "But then he found Jesus." Jeff made little quotes with his fingers when he said, "found Jesus." The two men chuckled.

"Yeah," Mickey chimed in. "They were nice. They fed us breakfast and offered us a place to stay if we were willing to work for them."

Chelle and I exchanged glances.

Cody asked, "Work? What kind of work?"

"They had people cooking and cleaning," Jeff replied. "They have guards . . . oh, and a bunch of hunters too. They had more meat than I've seen since before The Havoc."

I paused, taking it all in. "Hanson Inn, eh?"

"Yep." Mickey said. "It's out on the Garden Highway. By that duck restaurant."

"Why didn't you guys stay?" Cody asked.

Jeff raised his chin a little. "Because no one's gonna tell me what to do. I don't care how big he his. I don't want him and his little hip-hop buddies bossing me around."

"Yeah," Mickey added. "We're doing just fine out here on our own."

"Looks that way," I agreed cordially.

We thanked them again for the fair trade, whistled for Slippery, and took the river trail north.

"Wow," Cody said, as soon as we were out of earshot. "Bitter, weren't they?"

"Yeah," I quickly agreed, thinking about other things. "We've gotta check out this place."

The next day we connected with the Sacramento River and crept up the Garden Highway toward the airport. We passed The Rusty Duck restaurant, and eventually arrived at a strip of hotels.

There was no sign of people as we snuck past the first couple hotels. Eventually we saw the Hanson Inn from a distance. We crept closer and found a spot to lay down behind some dry brush in a field behind the hotel.

"Down, boy." I made Slippery lie down next to me. We pulled out some jerky and chewed as we laid in wait.

A huge iron fence with a rolling gate surrounded the compound. The fence was probably 10 feet high—something built before The Havoc. Lots of these hotels had these fences before The Havoc. I'm not sure why. But now they were being put to good use.

About three minutes later, we saw two armed men walking the inside perimeter of the fence. I counted to myself. They crossed the same point every six minutes.

After a couple hours, we moved to a different vantage point. This time we saw a little bit of activity on the south side of the building. Some people came out to check on a large garden, then went back inside the building.

A large black man came outside and talked with the guards for a minute, greeting them both with a friendly fist bump.

"I wonder if that's Shiv," Cody said. "He's huge!"

"Only one way to find out," I said. "Let's go introduce ourselves."

"Are you sure?" Cody asked.

"If they were nice to Jeff and Mickey, I think they'll be fine with us." I looked at Chelle. "Agreed?"

Chelle nodded. "I'm in."

I looked at Cody. "Cody?"

Cody thought for a moment and finally nodded. "Yeah. Let's check it out."

The three of us stood and began walking toward the hotel. It was only a matter of seconds before one of the armed men spotted us in the distance. He didn't look disturbed at all. He just leaned toward the other one and said something, nodding our way. The big man and the other guard led the way, walking toward us within the fence.

As we got within 100 yards, we put our hands in the air and

attempted to show a sign of submission. The men stopped just inside the gate and waited.

The three men were all very large, two of them black, one of them white. They were all dressed in T-shirts and jeans, typical for Sacramento in March. Their arms were chiseled and covered with jailhouse tats. The two guards, both smaller than the unarmed man, were by no means small. It's just that the unarmed man was huge! He was probably six foot seven and he had to weigh over 300 pounds.

When we were 10 yards from the gate, two men exited the door of the hotel, and that's what stopped us dead in our tracks. One of them was a face we recognized from the riverbank two years before.

Before I could even think it, Chelle quietly said, "Money."

The large black man saw the three of us standing there, and he tilted his head, confused. He turned around and saw Money approaching, and then he looked back at us.

As Money sauntered toward the gate, he noticed the large man's confusion and looked over at us. He connected eyes with me and stopped walking.

Everyone felt the tension, and both guards raised their guns at us.

Before anyone could respond, the large black man raised his hands and shouted, "Hold up, hold up! Nobody make a move!"

Time froze. I actually felt the hairs on the back of my neck sticking straight up. I didn't dare move a muscle with those two assault rifles pointed at us.

The man who walked out of the hotel definitely was Money;

I recognized those eyes. But he looked completely different. He wasn't wearing his prison garb, and he looked a little more groomed than the last time we'd seen him.

The large black man pointed to Money and then to us as he calmly said, "I can see that you all know each other. Is that correct?"

I reflected for a moment. I could almost feel the blow of the rifle butt to my cheek. "Yep. That man ripped off the three of us a few years back."

The black man turned to Money and asked him. "Is this true, Todd?"

Money didn't say a word. So Cody took the opportunity to jump in, "His name isn't Todd. His name is Money. And he owes me a knife!"

"Cody!" I quickly interjected. "You're not helping!"

"Todd," the black man said calmly, "did you take their stuff and this short one's knife?"

Money lowered his head a bit. He looked like a little kid caught with his hand inside the cookie jar. Then he looked up at the big man in charge. "It's true. I did it years ago when I was still running with my crew. And I struck that one," he said, pointing to me. "We took some stuff from their packs, but I honestly don't remember what."

Cody shook his head in disbelief.

Money looked at Chelle. "I do remember her."

The large man looked at us again. He seemed lost in thought for a moment, and then he said, "I want to apologize on behalf of my friend here." Looking directly at Cody he said, "Yes, he used to be called Money, but I call him by his real name now—Todd. And Todd helps me . . . " The man suddenly stopped mid-sentence, shook his head, and laughed. "I'm sorry. I haven't even introduced myself. I'm Shiv."

"How'd you get that name?" Cody asked.

Everyone, including Chelle and me, looked at Cody, like, *Really?*

Shiv laughed and said, "It's because I was so chivalrous. Whaddya think?"

Chelle turned to Money and said with a smile, "Todd, huh? I knew it wasn't too late for you."

Money smiled back. "About a year after I met you three, I ran into Shiv and his boys down at the Estuary at Discovery. I'd known Shiv from our time inside, but he was all different. I asked him what he was up to, and he told me he'd met Jesus.

"I thought he was kidding at first, but he wasn't. I've heard lots of fellas say that, just to get in good with the parole board and stuff. But they're always the same once they're back in the yard."

Money looked at Shiv and continued, "But not Shiv. He's different. He and his boys started this place, and they feed people who are hungry and need help. He's taken in a bunch of us and helped us—no matter what we've done. He said that's what Jesus would do."

"Amen," Shiv added.

Money walked closer to the gate and talked a little quieter, like he was telling us a secret. "I didn't believe it at first. But I thought this was a pretty cool place. I figured I'd fake it for a while, and then rip it off when I got a chance. But Shiv would take me with him to help others on the road, and I discovered I was actually good at it. It just felt right. So, I never got around to ripping him off," Money smirked.

"So now you're Todd," Chelle said.

Money smiled. "I'm Todd."

"Your mom would be proud."

Shiv opened the gate. "Let me give you guys a tour."

Slippery followed us through the gate. Shiv seemed to keep his distance from the dog.

"You don't like dogs?" Cody asked, noticing Shiv's apprehension.

"Most of the dogs I've met don't like black people. Especially big black people!"

"Well, I'll let you know if we see one," Chelle said, as Shiv opened the front door of the hotel.

Shiv smiled and looked at Money. "She's alright."

JOURNAL ENTRY #26

//

Something to Think About
Back to Reality . . .

• Would you have gone on the tour? Why or why not?

• Do you trust Money/Todd? Is his transformation legitimate?

• What changed Todd?

• Why does Shiv's life conversion seem so authentic?

THE BIBLE PROVIDES SOME GOOD WISDOM:

"Repent, then, and turn to God, so that your sins may be wiped out, that times of refreshing may come from the Lord." (Acts 3:19, NIV)

• The word repent in this verse means to literally stop going one way, turn 180 degrees, and start going the opposite way. Which way does this verse tell us to go?

• How do we turn around and begin walking toward God?

• According to the verse, what happens when we turn to God and our sins are wiped out?

• Describe the refreshment that Money/Todd experienced?

• What kind of refreshment might God have in store for you if you're willing to put your trust in him and follow him?

SOMETHING YOU CAN DO THIS WEEK:

What's stopping you from praying a prayer of repentance right now? If God is tugging at you heart, then try praying these three steps:

Dear God,
a. I really love you and thank you for . . .
b. I need your forgiveness. Please forgive me for . . .
c. I need to give you control. Please guide me, especially when . . .

Thank you for the refreshment you provide when we give you control!

UTOPIA

"Here's my room." Shiv showed us a small room on the bottom floor of the building. "It's the room closest to the front door. Me and most of the guards stay down here by the entrances and exits. People feel safer that way."

"What, you didn't want the suite on the top floor?" Cody asked.

"Yeah, it's pretty nice. But I gave that to Maria."

"Maria?" Chelle asked.

"Maria was working as a maid in this hotel when everything went to hell four years ago. She and a few of the cooks locked the gates and holed up in here. When Rich—one of the Folsom guards—let a few of us out, Maria's brother Miguel was worried about her. So I came over here with him to check on her and see if she was okay. She let us in, fed us, and gave us a place to stay. Over the years, we've taken in a whole crew of people. Maria serves all of them. She still cleans the rooms too. So it just seemed right that she should have the best room."

Shiv's appearance was intimidating, but his heart was soft.

I exchanged a quick glance with Chelle. I knew she would be evaluating the situation just like I was. We'd been looking for a place to call home for years now.

Could this be it?

Shiv brought us outside and showed us where they raise chickens. There was a huge pen with about 50 of them inside. Just outside the pen's gate, I told Slippery to stay, and then we stepped inside the pen.

dy began toying with the chickens. Shiv looked at Chelle. "Todd had a daughter about your age, you know? His old lady didn't let him see his kid. And she never visited him during his 14 years inside. He doesn't miss his old lady, but he sure misses his daughter."

Cody tired of chasing the chickens and joined us by the gate. "What's that?" he asked, pointing to what looked like a newly constructed barn. "That wasn't here when the hotel was still operating, was it?"

"Ha!" Shiv laughed. "No, I don't know of no Hanson Inn with a barn." He put up his hands playfully like a boxer and gave Cody a friendly jab in the arm. Then he dropped his guard and pointed to the barn. "That is the handiwork of Doug, our head of construction. He's all good with hammers and nails and stuff. We worked together and built that in less than a week. Gives us a place to keep the livestock when the weather's rough."

"Livestock?" I asked.

"Yeah. We've got only three cows right now, six horses, seven pigs, and thirteen goats."

"Milk," Chelle said, almost to herself.

"Yep. The cow milk is better than the goat milk. But we drink both."

Shiv showed us the garden. There were several rows of corn, strawberries, tomatoes, squash, watermelon, carrots, peas, and potatoes. He picked a couple of strawberries and handed them to us to munch on while we walked.

Eventually, he led us back toward the hotel. "Let me bring you in and introduce you to Jim. He's my pastor."

Shiv led us to a small conference room with about twelve chairs placed in a small circle. A tall, balding, white man with a kempt grey beard was talking with Money and another man. Money smiled when he saw Chelle walk into the room.

Chelle said, "It's good to see you're hanging out with better company now."

Todd chuckled. Gesturing toward his companions, he said, "Thus you will walk in the ways of the good and keep to the paths of the righteous."

It was a verbatim quote of Proverbs . . . from somewhere near the beginning of the book.

"Look at you, my brotha," Shiv said, giving Todd a hug. "All quotin' Scripture up in here."

Shiv turned to the man with the grey beard. "Jim, I want you to meet some new friends who just arrived. This is Chris, Cody, and Chelle."

Jim extended his hand and greeted us with a smile. "It's good to meet each of you."

He stepped back and looked us over. "Wow, you guys are young. Have you been surviving completely on your own?"

We nodded.

Jim's expression became solemn. "Parents?"

"Didn't make it," I answered quickly, not wanting to dwell on the subject.

"Hmm," Jim shook his head earnestly. "I'm really sorry to hear that. All of us here understand. There's not a person here who hasn't lost someone close. Tough times."

Shiv took the opportunity to change the subject. "Jim leads a Bible study in here each morning, and we also meet here for church on Sunday mornings and Wednesday nights."

Cody looked around the room. "Just 12 chairs?"

"Yeah," Shiv said, "it's just me, Todd, Jim, a few of my crew, and the family up in Room 312 who meet for the Bible study. And we get about 20 in here on Sunday mornings."

"How many live in this compound?"

"We have 47 people."

"Hey," Chelle offered, "20 people out of 47 going to church. That's a lot!"

"Yeah," Shiv continued, "People know my story. I was a gang-banger, a thief, and a murderer. But one day all my ways came back to stab me in the back . . . literally." Shiv turned around and raised his shirt. Amidst his carved muscles, he had a cluster of huge scars on the left side of his back. "Some fool shivved me seven times, hit my kidney, punctured a lung, and jacked me up big-time. I was lying in the prison hospital dying, and Jim came to visit me. Jim was the man who ran the art program up at Folsom. He'd met me only a few times. Anyway, I knew Jim was tight with God, so I asked if he could put in a good word for me. Jim told me to tell God myself. Long story short—we talked, I prayed, and I promised God that very day that if he let me live, I'd live for him."

He turned to Todd and laughed. "I never thought he'd take me up on it. I guess God's plans aren't our plans, you know what I'm sayin'?" Todd and Shiv held out their fists and gave each other a friendly pound.

"Anyway, people here know what I'm about. We offer church, but it's not required. We figure they'll see our good works and realize that it's not us, but God in us . . . feel me?" Shiv shrugged. "One by one, people are coming here more and more."

Jim put his hand on Shiv's shoulder. "Thanks to Shiv's leadership, we have a nice little community here. No one owns any room, livestock, or supplies. We share everything, other than a few personal items of sentimental value. We truly live like the Christians did in the days of the early church when they faced persecution and tough times."

"Been there," I added.

Shiv showed Cody, Chelle, and me to our rooms. Maria came in and greeted each of us, giving us clean bedding and towels.

There was one other dog on the compound, an Australian shepherd mix. It slept in its owner's room. Maria met Slippery and was fine with him staying in one of our rooms. We let him stay with Chelle.

As Maria left, the three of us gathered in Cody's room and sat on his bed. Cody felt the mattress and smiled.

"Whaddya think?" I asked.

Cody grinned bigger than I'd seem him smile in years. "He patted the bed with his left hand. I think I'm going to sleep well tonight."

I looked over at Chelle. "Chelle?"

"It's hard to make a quick judgment, but these look like really good people. Good enough to trust for a few nights anyway.

Time will tell. Time will tell."

An hour later, we went to our own rooms and unpacked our backpacks. It was a bizarre experience. I actually opened a dresser drawer and put a few of my dirty shirts away.

That's when I saw the pair of khaki shorts stuffed in the bottom of my pack. I pulled them out carefully and turned the front pocket inside out, exposing a glimmer of gold and a shimmering stone. Four years before, I'd carefully sewn my grandma's wedding ring into these shorts. It had seen daylight only a few times since that day. No one but Cody even knew about it.

I gave the ring a quick shine with my T-shirt, careful not to unfasten it from its hand sewn attachment.

I held it up to the sunlight streaming in the window. *You, my little friend, are going to be put to use very soon.*

I tucked the pocket back inside, rolled up the shorts, and buried them safely in the bottom of my pack.

That night the three of us slept better than we had since . . . I can't remember.

Tomorrow would be a big day.

FINAL JOURNAL ENTRY

///

Something to Think About
Back to Reality . . .

• Would you trust Shiv, Todd, and the people at the hotel? Would you stay the night?

• Chelle mentioned that they "looked like really good people." What specific evidence of their goodness did Cody, Chris, and Chelle see?

• Shiv showed his genuine faith in even the small things, like giving Maria the suite on the top floor. Is it smart for a leader to show this kind of servantlike attitude? Explain.

THE BIBLE PROVIDES SOME GOOD WISDOM:

"Jesus knew that the Father had given him authority over everything and that he had come from God and would return to God. So he got up from the table, took off his robe, wrapped a towel around his waist, and poured water into a basin. Then he began to wash the disciples' feet, drying them with the towel he had around him." (John 13:3-5, NLT)

• How did Jesus model leadership?

• What kind of example did Jesus set for how we should treat others?

• What are some ways you can serve or "wash the feet" of others this week?

SOMETHING YOU CAN DO THIS WEEK:

Choose someone whom you can serve this week: a family member, a friend, or a teacher. Think of a specific way you can serve that person, demonstrating a Christlike attitude. Set a reminder in your phone or on your calendar to help you do it.